MARQUESS OF MALICE

LORDS OF SCANDAL BOOK 2

TAMMY ANDRESEN

Keep up with all the latest news, sales, freebies, and releases by joining my newsletter!

www.tammyandresen.com

Hugs!

UNTITLED

Marquess of Malice
    Lords of Scandal Book 2

By Tammy Andresen

CHAPTER ONE

MALICE, as his friends fondly referred to him, sat on a bench in the garden of the Chase family home, staring at the newly emerging spring flowers sprouting from the ground.

His name was Lord Chadwick Hennessey, Marquess of Malicorn, but no one had called him by his given name since his mother had given it to him with her dying breath.

Which was likely why he hated being called Chadwick. It held too many ugly memories. He ran his hand through his hair, staring at a small green bud struggling to rise up through the dirt. He grimaced. He'd been that flower as a child. Struggling and straining to flourish, the very ground that was supposed to nurture him pushing him back into the dirt.

He straightened his back, drawing in a deep breath. He wasn't that child any longer. He was a grown man now who never wallowed in self-pity.

Standing, he stared down at the tiny plant. He wouldn't expend emotion on a flower but he could help it. Just a bit. He leaned over and brushed the dirt away from the small plant giving it more room to grow. Satisfaction spread through his limbs and he let out a long breath as more of the bright green stock came into view.

"Oh," a feminine voice trilled from his left. "My apologies, my lord."

He stopped, his fingers still in the dirt. He'd been caught caring about a tiny plant. Even worse, it was *her* who had made the discovery. His insides tightened. Despite the fact this was only the second time they'd met, he knew the sound of Lady Cordelia Chase's voice without even looking at her.

Malice had carefully fostered a reputation of reckless abandon sprinkled with a healthy dose of sarcastic indifference. He rarely showed emotion toward anyone or anything. He most definitely didn't want Lady Cordelia to think he was a sappy sort. It would give her the wrong impression. "What are you apologizing for?" Malice straightened, giving her a long look as he glared down at her. How odd.

She pushed up her glasses, nibbling at her lip.

"For interrupting. Had I known anyone was out here, I would have come with a chaperone."

He relaxed, his shoulders slumping down. She didn't seem to have noticed that he was aiding tiny plants. "No need to apologize." He cared not if she were chaperoned, despite the fact that she was a tender debutante. "How goes the wedding breakfast?"

Cordelia turned back to look at the house. "Very well. If you'll excuse me, I'll just return inside."

"No need." He waved his hand. "I'll escort you back to the wedding breakfast in just a moment."

She cocked her head to one side. "I beg your pardon?"

He ignored her question, instead studying her from top to bottom. Her fair hair was tied rather tightly back from her face. The hair itself looked soft and he wondered how she might look with a looser coif. Her glasses perpetually slid down her nose, likely because it was the tiniest nose he'd ever seen with just a slight upturn at the bottom. When she looked at him over the top of the glasses, her eyes were a striking color of crystal blue like a lake on a sunny day. Quite pleasant.

On their very first meeting, she'd not been wearing the spectacles and had promptly tripped into his arms. She had a nice figure. Curvy without being overly large, and without the dark rims of her glasses, he'd noted the lovely shape of her eyes, large and clear with a gentle upturn at the outside corners. Glasses or no, a man couldn't miss how nice the curve of her mouth was—so full and tempting.

He'd also realized she was a quiet and affable lady who would make an excellent wife.

Unlike many men, he'd made several decisions on that front. First, he planned never to fall in love. Emotions like that were an affliction. As the holder of the title, he was obligated to continue his line, by marrying and conceiving an heir. Not a part of his life he looked forward to.

His parents' marriage had been brief, to say the least. Barely a year. He didn't remember his mother, of course, but he couldn't imagine that the union had been a happy one, if his own relationship with his father was any indication. Although his father would swear that all the love he felt had died with his mother. "Tell me, Lady Cordelia. How do you spend your time?" He assumed reading, knitting, and socializing were at the top of her list. All excellent pastimes for a wife.

She shrugged, inching back a bit. "I don't know. What all ladies do. A little of this and a bit of that."

He stepped forward. Her comment highlighted what he liked about her. She appeared to be a malleable woman. Easy in her temperament, which was exactly the sort of woman he needed.

And that was the main reason he was here. Cordelia, along with her sisters, had arrived at their secret club in the middle of the night. But the ladies weren't supposed to be there. In fact, they weren't supposed to know about the club at all. Now one of his partners, the Earl of Effington, was married to Cordelia's sister, Emily.

When Emily had arrived with her two sisters, Cordelia and Grace, and her cousins, Minnie and Diana, all hell had broken loose. The men were concerned about the club's secret, the ladies about their reputations. Emily and Jack had almost called off the wedding. And the other men had begun to fear for their club's reputation and continued business. They'd made a thriving, financially successful gaming hell by creating an air of mystery about their identities. To make certain this continued, Malice and his friends had decided to watch the ladies and make certain they didn't share their secret.

"Sounds delightful," he said, his thoughts still on their first meeting a few weeks prior.

When Cordelia had nearly fallen directly into his arms, she'd blushed and apologized. He'd held her close, taken off her domino, and studied her face. She was pretty, petite, almost pixie-like. Quiet and unassuming. He'd decided right then. He'd marry her, make an heir, and settle her into his country estate leaving her to raise the child. Easy.

She squinted her eyes. "Really? I was thinking a little of this and a bit of that didn't sound like anything at all."

He looked back at her, his mind refocusing to the present. Was the sun reflecting off her glasses or was there a glint in her eye? "Precisely."

Her small pink tongue darted from her mouth and licked her full upper lip, starting in one corner and sliding across the entire bow of her mouth until it finally finished on the opposite side. His insides tightened in the strangest way. He knew what lust was, he was a seasoned man of eight and twenty. He'd had more than his fair share of partners. But Cordelia should have nothing to do with such emotions. Why was his body responding to her? She was the safe and predictable choice.

He'd chosen her so that he'd have a wife from whom he could remain detached.

"What do you mean, precisely? Precisely what? That doesn't make sense. You don't want me to say anything of consequence?" She narrowed her gaze. "Why do you care what I say at all?"

He frowned. They were already getting off topic. "You're missing the point."

"I don't think I am." She curtseyed. "Now, if you'll excuse me." Lady Cordelia gave a small sniff and then she turned to go.

Malice dropped his hands, his brow scrunching. What the bloody hell was she doing? Letting out a frustrated breath he crossed the garden and grabbed her arm.

———

CORDELIA STARTED DOWN THE PATH, determined to leave the Marquess of Malicorn where he belonged —in her past.

It wasn't that she didn't like him, precisely. He was darkly handsome with a square jaw and features that were disconcerting in their sharpness. Prominent cheek bones and a heavy brow that lent him an air of danger.

She shivered, despite herself. His large frame hinted at muscles that surely were a hazard to any upstanding lady. Both because she knew him to be a man that didn't follow rules and because all his features put together, made him rather...exciting.

As if he were reading her thoughts, he reached out and wrapped his fingers about her arm at the same time he spoke her name. "Lady Cordelia."

She jolted, her insides going silly as she whirled about. "You frightened me."

He immediately dropped his hand. "My apologies. I simply would like to continue our conversation."

Cordelia caught her lip between her teeth. "Very kind of you, but I must decline."

He stared down at her, his brows drawing together. She'd thought his eye color was near black but out here in the light, she could see they were far more chocolate in their shade of brown and rather endearing. "Why?"

Her mouth opened as she tried to form words. Why? Was it not obvious? "You are an eligible man and I am an eligible woman. We should not be found alone together. We've enough scandal floating about us already. You know the Countess of Abernath has threatened to expose me and my family for our visit to your club. We should take every precaution to be proper."

He relaxed at those words, his shoulders easing down. "I agree and I appreciate your sense of propriety. It's a most advantageous quality."

Cordelia stilled, his words tumbling about her mind. There it was again. He was complimenting her on some attribute that he found pleasing. Why? "You like my propriety and my hobbies that I haven't even named. Which actually makes no sense."

His brow dropped low, his mouth pinching into a frown. "You're smarter than I thought you'd be."

"Thank you?" she said, giving her head a small shake.

He waved. "No matter." Then he reached out to her again, taking her hand in his. Even with her gloves on, a tingly sort of sensation travelled up her arm. "What I wish to discuss with you would solve all of your problems with the countess and with propriety and so on and so forth."

She lifted an eyebrow. "Why do I get the impression that I want to know the details of the so on and so forth?"

His mouth pulled to one side. "You ask a lot of questions."

"Again. Thank you." The tingling was growing distracting and so she pulled her hand from his. Then she bobbed another quick curtsy. "If that is all, my lord."

"No." He crossed his arms. "That isn't all."

She suppressed a sigh. He clearly wasn't going to gracefully allow her to leave until he'd said whatever he was hinting around. "Pray, continue."

He swallowed, his Adam's apple bobbing. "As a marquess there are certain duties that I need filled."

"Duties?" Oh dear. There was only one reason a lord wished to speak to a lady about his duties and that was when he wanted her to fulfill one of them for him by giving him a child. Cordelia cleared her throat, pressing her hand to her stomach.

"Yes." He stepped a bit closer and she moved back. The frown lines on his forehead deepened. "I am in need of a wife and child to ensure that my line and legacy continue. I think that you'd make an excellent candidate. Not only would you be helping me secure my future but I, in turn, could protect you from any scandal."

"Scandal you're creating now by the two of us being here alone?" she asked, taking another step back. The Marquess of Malicorn was not a suitable candidate for her. Not only was he mysteriously dangerous, but he engaged in questionable pastimes.

He scoffed, the smell of the cigar he'd surely just smoked filling her nostrils. She'd always liked the scent. It was earthy with a bit of cherry. "I mean you coming into a part of town you weren't supposed to be in and then stumbling into the back room of a gentleman's club." He lowered his head. "The countess knows sensitive information about you."

Cordelia placed her other hand over her heart. "Are all your friends going to propose to my sisters and cousin?" Point in fact, Minnie had just married the Duke of Darlington and the Earl of Exmouth had seemed quite interested in her sister, Diana. Was this a group plan?

He raised his hands up. "What does that have to do with anything?"

"I'm just trying to determine your motivations. Your sudden proposal is quite a surprise."

He pinched the bridge of his nose with his thumb and two fingers. "Perhaps my first impression of you was incorrect."

"Oh, this should be interesting. Tell me, what did you think of me?" Butterflies flitted in her stomach exposing her lie. She wasn't entirely certain she wanted to know.

He dropped his hands. "That you'd be a suitable wife. I wished to speak with you to ask you to marry me."

"But you no longer wish to ask?" That was beside the point. She didn't want to marry him either. "And what about me precisely seemed suitable?" Even the word suitable made her heart sink. Diana was bold and daring. Minnie was strong and fiery. Grace was beautiful beyond compare and Ada was angelic. But Cordelia, the word burned in her brain. She was suitable. It wasn't that she hadn't known her entire life she was the least of all her cousins and sisters. But she'd hoped, perhaps foolishly, to find a man who thought her more. In fact, it had been the one dream that had carried her through a childhood where she was often unseen, surrounded by so many beautiful women.

"You're not so loud and brash. You have manners, you seem quiet and—"

"Please, Lord Malicorn. That's enough." She held up her hand. "Much as I appreciate your offer for a *suitable* match. I simply must decline."

"What?" He reached for her arm again, but she was quick enough to step back this time. She wouldn't be caught by him again.

Taking a breath, she notched her chin as Diana or Minnie would do. "You heard me, my lord. My answer to your proposal is no."

CHAPTER TWO

THE LITTLE IMP spun about and raced down the path leaving Malice to stand there with his bloody mouth gaping open. "She said no," he repeated to no one in particular. A garden bird answered, calling merrily as though to mock him. He was a marquess, for Christ's sake. Women didn't say no to marquesses, did they?

Recovering his senses, he stalked after her. Did he want to catch her? He wasn't so certain. Actually, he was beginning to regret his proposal entirely.

He supposed he should have gotten to know her better but that was the point. Malice didn't want to know her. He wished to bed her and then ship her off. Complete his duty without ever feeling a thing.

The very fact that she'd poked at his motivations and then fled told him what he needed to know. She wasn't the woman for him. A little disappointment made him rub the back of his neck. Part of him had been looking forward to the bedding.

Which was ridiculous. He could find another woman that was little and blonde with a small pink tongue and…he slashed his hand through the air. He didn't need a replacement for Cordelia. He didn't need her at all, well except for the part where she conceived an heir.

But if she didn't want the position, he'd find another woman to fill the role. One who didn't ask so many bloody questions.

He stormed back up the steps and through the front door of the Chase home. He'd say goodbye to his friend, Daring, the Duke of Darlington, and leave this place, never to return. He didn't need Lady Cordelia Chase, he'd been doing her a favor, after all.

But he didn't have a chance to return to the wedding breakfast. Daring was standing in the foyer with his arms crossed over his chest. "What the bloody hell do you think you are doing?" Daring had a deep voice and it echoed up the vaulted ceilings, reaching the intricately painted cherubs that graced the entry. The Lord of Winthrop was an earl and a rich one at that.

Malice stopped, assessing his friend. "Coming to say goodbye."

"And where were you just now?"

Malice let out a groan of frustration. "What is it with all the questions today?"

Daring took a step closer, his body tensed like a bear or a wolf. His chest was puffed out and his teeth showed in the morning light. "Just one more question. Were you alone in the garden with Cordelia?"

Malice gave Daring a sidelong glance. The answer, of course, was yes. "I asked her to marry me, if you must know."

Daring didn't relax as Malice had expected. In fact, his fists clenched at his sides. "Then why did she come in here crying?"

Malice tossed up his hands again. "You want me to explain women? A complete bluestocking rejected me and I'm supposed to know why she's upset?"

Daring didn't say another word as he charged at Malice. Knowing what was coming, Malice ducked just as the other man's large fist swung at his head. "For feck's sake," he swore as he dodged another beefy fist.

Daring pushed him instead of answering, sending Malice crashing into the door. He could hit back at his friend but he wouldn't.

"Did you not hear yourself? A bluestocking rejected you and you can't understand why?" Daring stepped up so that his face was inches from Malice's.

"You don't like or respect her. She's a kind and gentle woman, but she's not stupid."

Malice grimaced. That was a valid point. And he had figured that out all on his own. Without being punched, even. Especially the part about her being quite smart. "I'm not interested in a romantic marriage. Is it so wrong that I didn't lie to her and tell her falsehoods?"

The contours of Daring's face softened. "No, that's not wrong. But you hurt her feelings and you're going to make that right."

Malice frowned as he looked Daring in the eye. "Is that absolutely necessary?"

"Yes," Daring growled back. "Consider it your wedding present to me." Then he shoved Malice back into the door. "You couldn't have picked a different day to ask her?"

That made Malice wince. "I'd thought she'd say yes."

Daring shook his head. "Didn't you learn by watching me? These Chase women hold their own."

"Point taken," Malice answered as he slid out from Daring's pin against the door. "I'll apologize. *I'm sorry I asked you to marry me.*"

Daring narrowed his gaze. "That's not what you're apologizing for."

reading had blossomed into a desire to write. She'd began her own stories. Not of romance, of course. She didn't fully understand the subject, if she were honest. But she'd written stories of children. Tales of the forgotten child, the less pretty one, the broken birds whose wings needed to be healed.

Ada, her cousin, held her hand on her other side. "He's a little frightening anyway."

Cordelia raised a brow. She supposed Malice was a bit intimidating. In fact, she was scared of him too. Not because of his looks or his demeanor but because of her physical reaction to him. He effortlessly made her heart thump wildly. He was the sort of man who would normally be interested in Diana or Grace. Not Cordelia. She dropped her head at the thought. "Why do you think that?"

"His eyes are intense and his features so…strong. He reminds me of a hawk who swoops down and eats little birds in the garden." Ada gave a small shiver.

Grace shrugged from her seat across from Cordelia. "I think he's handsome."

Minnie, who was next to her, poked Grace's arm.

Grace cringed in pain, then reached over and patted Cordelia's knee. "But obviously a cad." Then Grace straightened. "What did he say to disturb you so?"

Cordelia pressed her lips together. This was tricky. Did she share with them that the Marquess had proposed? If her mother or aunt found out, she might find herself hastily engaged. Both had an eye for an eligible man who was titled. "Well, that's an interesting question."

Diana's ceased her rhythmic comforting motion. "How so?"

Drat. Cordelia pressed her hands together. "Well, he said that I was suitable, and that he needed a wife for childbearing."

Her family reacted to her words with complete silence. Licking her lips, she went on. "Then he asked for my hand in marriage. When I refused, he confessed that he'd had the wrong impression of me, he'd thought me less intelligent and more docile."

"That man is a piece of horse's dung," Diana said, her lips thinning over her teeth. "What sort of proposal is that?"

Grace straightened her skirts. "Dreadful."

Cordelia sighed with relief. "Don't tell mother, or anyone else, especially not auntie." She looked over at Ada. "You know how your mother can be about a perceived good match."

Ada nodded. "I certainly won't."

"Still, Corde, you can be glad for one thing."

Grace shifted in her seat. "You managed to get a proposal, even a bad one, before either me or Diana."

Cordelia shrugged. Grace was trying to help, which she really appreciated. "When you get a proposal Grace, it will be because some man is so taken with you, that he'll wish to sweep you off your feet. For me? I got one because I am *suitable*." The word tasted bitter in her mouth.

"Well, that is interesting to know. The next time I propose to a woman I'll shall make sure to leave that word out of it entirely."

Cordelia froze. Just her eyes moving so that she might look at the door. Of course, the Marquess of Malicorn stood in the entry of the room, his back straight as an arrow as he assessed her. Drat. He'd heard every word and what was worse, they'd likely need to talk about it.

CHAPTER THREE

MALICORN SQUEEZED the outside of his thigh. How had this day gone so wrong?

Cordelia slowly stood from her spot on the couch, folding her hands across her stomach. "Wise choice, my lord."

"I didn't mean to offend," he said as one by one the ladies stood. "I only meant that you have the qualities I am looking for in a wife."

Daring was just behind him and Malice drew in a deep breath to keep his face from heating. Did this conversation have to be witnessed by so many people?

She gave a small curtsy. "I appreciate your explanation. I only wish to respond that while it is a very generous offer, I believe that I am looking for different qualities in a match than you are."

Her face turned a lovely shade of pink as she looked at the floor. His body tightened in awareness. How had he not noticed how creamy her complexion was? "Do tell, Lady Cordelia. What are you looking for in a husband?" He closed his eyes wondering why he'd just asked that question. He only meant to apologize.

Then he opened them. Which was a mistake because she was doing that thing with her tongue again. The one he liked. He had a sudden picture of following the path along her lips with his own tongue.

She stepped forward. "It's not important."

He lowered his chin, studying her. Their first meeting, he had liked her deference in these situations. But now, it appeared to be more of a deflection. She didn't speak because she didn't want to talk to him. "Your wishes are important to me."

He heard a woman gasp. He didn't look to see which one, it didn't matter to him if the lady wasn't Cordelia.

She fluffed out her skirts, staring at the floor. "I suppose I want a man who shares my interests and—"

He raised a finger. "To be fair, I asked you what your interests were. You gave a very vague answer."

Her chin snapped up then, and she stared at him

23

over her glasses. Reaching up, she pulled them from her face then pointed them at him. "To be fair, you were glad when I didn't really answer." Her chin notched. "Which is to my point. Not only do I want a husband who shares my likes and dislikes but I'd prefer that he actually liked me." She tossed the glasses aside, taking a step forward. "I know I'm not much compared with my sisters but—"

His mouth dropped open and suddenly he understood. He had his own reasons for wanting a marriage of complete convenience and they were rooted in his past. Was it so odd that she needed a man to fill in her insecurities? "The rest of society will think you're wildly successful for having married a marquess."

She gave her head a tiny shake. "I'm sure they would."

The pink in her cheeks spread down her neck. The shade of color reminded him of pink dogwood blossoms in the spring. The very same ones in the tree he'd hidden in as a child.

"But you wouldn't." He drew in a long breath. It was better she'd said no. He was already growing strangely sentimental over the girl. "Very well. I hope that I've apologized for my gaffe in manners."

She gave him a small smile. The sort that crinkled her eyes and highlighted the apples of her cheeks. "No need to apologize. I wouldn't have expected anything less from a man named Malice."

Her accusation made him stiffen. The name was fine among his male friends, but he didn't like hearing her say it. Did she think him cruel? Was that part of the reason she'd declined? He clenched and unclenched his fist. What did it matter? This would all be made easier if he could simply leave.

Unfortunately, he couldn't just bid Cordelia farewell. He'd agreed to keep watch over the little nymph before him. Until such time he was certain she wouldn't share the club's secrets or be ruined, he'd have to keep an eye on her.

"Corde," one of the women hissed. "We're not supposed to use that name."

Corde. He liked it. Something about it suited her fairy-like features. He had this brief flash of her flying over him and sprinkling him with her magic dust. He gave his head a shake. "I would also prefer you not use that name but as we're all familiar with it here, there's no harm."

"All right," Daring muttered behind him, letting out a long breath. "You're acting very strange."

He ignored Daring, focusing on Cordelia instead. She'd folded her hands over her stomach. "Minnie." She looked to her cousin. "Shouldn't we return to your wedding breakfast? Surely you and Lord Darlington are anxious to begin your travel."

"That's very thoughtful of you," Darlington called from behind her, "But we're only travelling across London." He stepped next to Malice, squeezing part of his body in the door frame. "Why don't you ladies return to the breakfast? Lord Malicorn and I will be along momentarily."

Daring slapped him on the shoulder, hard. Then he pushed him into the room so the ladies could get out. They filed past silently, each giving him a side-long glance before exiting. He crossed his arms and straightened his back.

Cordelia, the final lady to pass, stopped just in front of him. She drew in a deep breath. "Thank you, Lord Malicorn."

"For what?" he asked, cocking his head as he studied her.

She stepped a little closer. "For asking for my hand." Her eyes darted everywhere but toward him. "I haven't had much male attention in my life but forever I get to say I got a proposal before Diana or Grace. Not an easy task to be certain." Then she smiled and stared into his eyes. "Thank you for asking me instead of one of them."

His chest tightened. He wished he could reach out and touch her face. Trail his thumb along the delicate curve of her cheek while he leaned over and softly kissed the plump curve of her mouth. "You're welcome." Then he cleared his throat, crossing the room and picking up her spectacles. "Don't forget these."

He brought them back to her, their fingers brushing as he placed the frames in her hand. Waves of tension passed through him at the touch. She was very pretty without her glasses. Beautiful even, but somehow, he liked the spectacles on her face even more. With a final nod, she turned and followed the other women from the room.

"That's it," Daring said from just next to him. "Tell me what the bloody blue bullocks is going on with you."

"With me? You're the one who keeps pushing and shoving me." He turned to his friend, cocking a brow. "Love doesn't look all that pretty on you."

"See." Daring poked him in the chest. "That's the man I know. Sarcastic quips instead of polite manners or even actual feelings." Daring stepped closer. "And another thing, when do you allow me to take a swing at you without hitting back? When do you freely hand out apologies and then give ladies permission to use your secret name? When do you pick up objects for people from the floor? I'd have expected you to step on them after her rejection."

Malice shrugged, fixing his gaze on the wall to his right. "I am capable of change. I have to marry and, if nothing else, I've realized I may have to soften a bit to get a woman to agree. I was testing the theory and it seemed to have worked." Liar. He'd smoothed his rougher edges because he'd been worried about Cordelia's feelings. Him, the Marquess of Malice, being considerate. It was beyond ridiculous.

And Daring couldn't know that. His friend had just fallen in love and gotten married. If Daring found out that Malice was even a little mushy on a woman he'd start getting ideas about love matches and happy endings. He'd tell Minnie and Minnie would share with Cordelia. Then Cordelia might have entirely inappropriate ideas about what to expect from him.

Not that she was marrying him. She'd been rather firm in her rejection. But, despite his wounded pride and the realization she wasn't quite the woman he'd thought, he also wasn't ready to give up. What he needed now was a plan.

———

CORDELIA STOOD by the smoked salmon plate on the banquet table, her head bent with Grace and Diana's.

They were supposed to be enjoying Minnie's wedding breakfast. Instead they were...scheming. "So you're absolutely certain the Countess of Abernath will be at the Regal Ball?"

"She never misses it," Grace said as she fluffed her skirts. "And my friend, Amelia, heard her discussing it with her maid at the sweet shop on Baker Street."

"Your friend heard?" Diana sniffed. "Is that really enough to go on?"

"Oh please." Grace waved. "You want to go whether she's there or not."

"Why are we seeking out the countess again?" Cordelia's stomach clenched. "She threatened to ruin us. Do we really want to give her the venue to do so?"

Minnie joined them, her features set in a deep frown. "Are we discussing the countess? She doesn't need you to be present to ruin you, Corde. In fact, it would be easier for her to just start a rumor when we're not in attendance."

That was true. "She strikes me as a woman with a fair bit of gall. She'd prefer a large public display."

"Fair point." Diana nodded. "I simply want to test her. Is she going to call us out publicly? If she doesn't then I say we can relax and go about our lives."

Diana took her hand. "But I'll go without you three. No need for you to suffer as well."

Cordelia shook her head. She couldn't do that to Diana. "No. I'll come with you." Then she turned to Grace who was staring at the fish. "Grace?"

Her sister didn't look up. "Must we all be ruined on the same night?"

"Grace," she and Diana said in the same moment.

"Fine." Grace sighed. "I'll come." Then she glanced over at Minnie. "Can you and Darlington escort us? You are married now. If I'm going to be ruined, I'd prefer Mother not be in attendance."

Minnie gave a stiff nod. "Of course. Who better to understand what the countess is doing than my husband? But Mother may go anyway. You know how she is about these things."

Diana brushed her forehead with her hand. "If the countess chooses to ruin us then Mother will find out no matter what."

Cordelia winced. Once upon a time, Darlington had been engaged to the now Countess of Abernath. The relationship had ended so badly that Darlington hadn't pursued another woman for years until he met Minnie. The Countess harbored some deep anger that she directed toward anyone that Darlington cared about. "Have you factored into this plan the fact that the countess is likely stark-raving mad?"

Diana straightened. "She doesn't frighten me."

"That makes one of us," Grace mumbled.

Darlington and Malice entered the room again and crossed over to where the ladies stood. Tendrils of energy zipped through Cordelia as Malice approached. She looked down, carefully studying the carpet until he disappeared from her peripheral view.

"What are we discussing?" Darlington asked with a smile as he placed his arm about his new bride.

Minnie gave him a tight smile. "A ball my cousins are hoping we can escort them to."

Darlington's eyes narrowed. "Of course we can, but I'm curious to know why everyone looks as though we're going to a funeral instead of a ball."

Cordelia sucked in a breath. They'd been caught. She took a step back, not sure she wanted to participate in this conversation. The day had been full of drama as it was. But as she moved she bumped into a solid mass behind her. "Oh. I'm sorry." She spun, already suspicious about who was positioned at her back. But her skirts tangled in her legs and her foot knocked some boot and then she tumbled to the side.

A squeak erupted from her lips just as a large

hand caught her in midair. As quickly as she'd been falling, she was righted again.

"You make a habit of falling in my presence," Malice rumbled, his hand still firmly holding her rib cage.

She tried to pull away, discreetly of course, but his hand was far stronger than her small attempt to move. And besides, something about his large hand was rather comforting as they discussed Lady Abernath. "You make a habit of tripping me."

He gave a low chuckle, the sound echoing through her.

"Don't make him feel bad for catching you," Grace clucked. "You've always been unsteady on your feet. It's your vision."

Cordelia's nails dug into her palm. Cordelia had never, in her entire life, wanted to pull Grace's hair more.

By way of answer, Malice reached up and adjusted Cordelia's glasses on her nose, pushing them more firmly onto her face. "These things are too big for your tiny nose."

Cordelia shrugged. "I should likely get a new pair."

"We've gotten off topic," Daring cut in. "The ball?"

either. Even worse was the idea of someone asking. His blood boiled at the thought of another man waltzing with her in the ballroom.

"Oh, yes. Of course." She cleared her throat. "Did you have a particular dance in mind?"

"This one," he answered, taking her hand and threading it through his elbow to pull her out on the floor.

Her fingers rested delicately on his arm. Mistakenly, he glanced over and caught a hint of cleavage out of the top her wide-necked gown. His body clenched and he drew in a deep breath.

"My lord," she said moving closer so her hip brushed his.

His damn cock jumped to attention. This wasn't how it was supposed to be. Cordelia was always meant to be the bride he didn't give a wit about. Now he worried for her feelings, while his insides were hectic with attraction. When had that happened? He blamed that damn little tongue.

As if she'd read his mind, the thing darted out, her fingers digging more deeply into his arm. "Thank you for asking me to dance."

"There is no need," he replied.

She touched his other arm. "You and I both know that there is a need." She cleared her throat. "I've gone back and forth, in my mind, about whether I made the right decision saying no to you. Perhaps yours is my only offer. Maybe I'm just not the sort of woman who gets love and romance."

Bile rose in his throat along with words of protest. He swallowed them down. He'd wanted to disagree and tell her that she should hold out for a man who saw how special she was. But he clenched his teeth. He'd never make her feel that way, he didn't want to or know how.

What he should do, was ask her to marry him again. In this moment of weakness, she'd likely say yes. Then he'd have what he'd wanted from the start. But somehow, he couldn't subject her to emotional manipulation, either. She'd been the summer breeze of honest fresh air this ball had desperately required.

What he'd be taking away from her...

"Do you know what I admire about you?" he asked.

She looked over to him, her gaze wary. "I couldn't say."

He wanted to start by telling her all the places on his body he'd like that tongue to lick and all the parts he'd lick in return. But that wasn't what she needed. "Your honesty." He found a spot on the dance floor and turned to her, taking her in his arms.

Her lips pursed. "That's very kind."

"I'm not being kind." He began to spin her about

the room. "My mother died in childbirth while having me. My father, I believe, secretly hated me because of it. He'd never admitted it of course." He heard her gasp, but he kept going, somehow needing to say this. "But a person can feel when another doesn't like him. When we were in public, he'd hug me. Pat my head. But in the privacy of our own home," Malice gave a shiver. "It was a different story."

She squeezed his forearm. "Oh, Lord Malicorn."

But Malice shook his head. An overwhelming urge to tell her more of the truth rose up inside him. But he couldn't do it here in front of everyone. And when he told her, he wanted her to say something more comforting than *Lord Malicorn*. He wanted her to call him by his given name. "My name is Chad…"

———

CHAD. She whispered the name, simply testing it in her mouth. It felt nice, the way her tongue touched the back of her teeth.

He was spinning them with an efficiency that left her breathless and she barely had time to register where they were before they slid out the doors, cool night air touching her skin.

The night was still young and few guests had

sought repose in the garden, making it easy for Malice to pull them onto a dark path.

Without a word, she found herself pressed against his body, the hard edges of him stealing her breath.

"Say my name again."

"You heard me?" she gasped as he trailed his hand down her spine.

What was happening? She'd had a great many fantasies about romantic interludes in the garden but none of them had been this exciting. How odd. His proposal had been all business but his touch...

"I did, now say it, please, Cordelia."

And then, heaven help her, he dropped his lips to the hollow of her neck and placed a light kiss on the skin. She felt as though she'd been struck by lightning as a bolt of pleasure shot through her. "Chad," she said, his name sounding breathless and wanton.

He groaned in response even as his lips slid up the column of her neck until they reached her ear. "This is the opposite of what I wanted from you," he said, his voice vibrating against her skin.

"I'm not sure I understand." She leaned her head to the side to give him better access.

"I used the word suitable, Cordelia. I wanted a wife not a lover." He gave her earlobe the smallest lick before he sucked it into his mouth.

Her insides turned to jelly. "I like this far better I think."

He began kissing across her cheek, his lips placing a small kiss on the corner of her mouth. "Would you trade secret kisses in the garden for my marriage proposal?"

"Yes," she replied without a second thought. "Most definitely yes."

"Ask and you shall receive." Then he covered her mouth with his.

She'd read more than a few books where the heroine received a kiss from the hero. She'd even attempted to write a scene such as this. But nothing had prepared her for the feel of his mouth nibbling at hers. The pressure of his lips as he kissed hers, first closed and then open, made her knees weak. When his tongue slid lightly against hers, she clutched his shoulders, the flood of tingly sensation making it difficult to stand or breathe or do anything but hold on.

Dimly, she was aware that he'd insinuated this kiss meant that he'd rescinded his marriage proposal. She didn't care. This was so much better than suitable.

She had no idea how much time had passed but vaguely she became aware of a change in sound.

Rather than music, she heard the stillness of the night and the sound of voices.

"Damn," Malice muttered against her lips. "The dance is done."

"Dance?" she asked pulling back a bit, her mind a jumbled mess.

He smiled in the dark and then lightly kissed her lips again, sliding his hands around her face to hold her cheeks. "This conversation isn't finished."

"This conversation never started," she answered, attempting to blink away the confusion.

He chuckled. "Oh, we said a great deal, I think."

"And yet I am more confused than ever," she said as he tucked her hand into the crook of his arm.

He looked this way and that, then pulled them from the shadows out into the light. Crossing swiftly to the patio doors, they stepped inside. "I'd like to say I could provide clarity, but I'm not certain I can."

"Tell me one thing." She stopped and looked over at him. "Did you rescind your offer of marriage?"

He frowned, looking down at her. "How could I rescind what you've already rejected?"

Cordelia's mouth fell open. "I suppose that's true."

"You, Lady Cordelia Chase," he leaned down close to her ear, "are stealing kisses in the garden and rejecting marriage proposals from marquesses."

A shiver of delight danced down her spine. She snapped her open mouth closed and swallowed. Had he just done that for her? Had he inserted romantic innuendo into this night? She didn't even care if he'd meant it or not. It was the greatest gift anyone had ever given her. And now she knew. There was a soft side to the Marquess of Malice after all. "Thank you for that."

He started walking again and she allowed him to lead her, her thoughts swirling about. He'd asked her, just before he'd kissed her, if she'd trade the proposal for the kiss. She hadn't hesitated and she didn't regret her choice. But she had a feeling, he was unlikely to ask again.

For whatever reason he didn't want to marry a woman he kissed in the garden. He only wanted one who was suitable.

A little remorse niggled in her belly. If she'd known the kiss was going to be like that, she might have said yes to the marriage and then stolen the kiss.

Still, it was her first real taste of romance and she'd not tarnish it with second thoughts.

Regret was for the morning.

CHAPTER FIVE

MALICE PULLED Cordelia closer in the crowd, wishing he could take her back out to the garden. Daring, however, would have none of that. If Malice didn't get Cordelia back promptly at the end of the set, Daring would be swinging at his face again, and this time, the duke wouldn't miss. Not only that, but Malice would find himself marching down the marriage aisle.

He looked over at Cordelia, trying to discern how he felt about that. He'd taken her out to the garden to tell her more of his story, an oddity in and of itself, and he'd ended up using their time to kiss her senseless.

Pleasure sizzled along his skin. What a kiss. He struggled to remember a time when he'd ever had a touch that had been so intimate. And somehow, that same urge to pull her against him again. He dug his fingers into his thigh. He was damaged enough and couldn't get attached to Corde now. He needed to put some distance between himself and Lady Cordelia Chase.

———

CORDELIA TOOK a steadying breath as she stepped next to her sister. Breathing, the most natural occurrence in the world, suddenly felt odd. She would have sworn that her own lungs had fallen into rhythm with Chad's.

She blinked, staring over at him. He was gripping his thigh in a way that made her wonder if he was having the same trouble she was? Somehow, she doubted it.

But Cordelia did feel a certain inspiration to write. She'd only written children's stories, but now…perhaps she could finally tackle a romance.

She didn't know how her story might end, but she did have a clear vision of the beginning. And in her story the hero would propose because he'd fallen madly in love. And her heroine would say yes, and then they'd share a magical kiss.

Then she bit her lip. Stories were only interesting if they had a few complications. Troubles to overcome. What would her characters suffer from? Surely not a botched proposal and an illicit kiss?

Those thoughts actually made her smile before she frowned again. This wasn't a complication in a happy story. The man's name was Malice. He wasn't her Prince Charming she'd dreamed of, she had to remember that fact.

Except as she studied the lines of his face, her heart sped up again, thrumming in her chest.

"Hello, Lady Cordelia. Lady Diana, good to see you," A female voice called from their right.

Cordelia turned to see the hostess of the event, Lady Wilson. "My lady." Cordelia dipped into a quick curtsy. "Thank you for much for having us."

"Thank you for coming." The other women grinned. "How is your sister faring in her new marriage?"

They'd managed to keep Emily's elopement a secret. All of London believed she'd married as planned. "Very good, my lady." Diana answered. "They're off on a celebratory journey."

"How delightful. Your parents must be looking forward to matching the rest of you in equally advantageous marriages."

Cordelia nibbled at the inside of her cheek to keep from answering. Her sister had only just

His lips pulled tighter, making the lines of his face even harder. "Excellent. May I request a waltz?"

Cordelia heard Malice make a noise deep in his throat as he stepped closer to them. Cordelia couldn't refuse. It would be rude beyond belief. "Of course," she managed to stutter.

"I'll see you at the next waltz then." With a final flourish, Lord McKenzie turned and left.

Lady Wilson stood next to them watching his departure. "How curious. I thought he was interested in—" Then she looked at Lady Cordelia and stopped. "But you, my dear, may end up the belle of this ball."

Cordelia drew in an unsteady breath. That didn't seem right at all.

CHAPTER SIX

MALICE STARED at Lord McKenzie's retreating back and contemplated how he might dismantle the man. He'd start with the fingers…

He squeezed his fist together, cracking a few knuckles. It wasn't just that the man had asked Cordelia to dance. That was likely a lie, but he ignored the truth. Mostly, he objected to the look in the man's gaze. Reminded him of a wolf. Malice grimaced. Did he have that same look?

Inwardly, he winced. He might. Cordelia brought out something both emotional and yet primal within him.

If that man thought he'd steal his own garden kiss, Lord McKenzie had another thing coming. Malice didn't know where he stood on his proposal, or his future with Cordelia, but he knew some

CORDELIA DREW IN A DEEP BREATH, wishing she'd had a bit more time between sets. Lord McKenzie danced as she would expect, with clean, crisp lines that spoke of beauty but they left little room for rest. And there was nothing intimate or soft in his embrace. Unlike the Marquess she'd rejected.

She caught Chad stalking through the crowd of bystanders to her right, his eyes on them even as Lord McKenzie spun her around so that she lost sight of her not-quite suitor.

By all accounts, McKenzie would be cast in the role of hero. But for her, the sight of Chad helped her relax a bit. He was the one who made her feel safe.

"Lord McKenzie, I've not seen you at many events. Do you attend often?"

He shook his head, staring down at her. "I'm not one to participate in society." He pulled her just a touch closer and she found herself resisting the tug, attempting to keep space between them.

"I understand. Society can be..."

"Exhausting." He filled in with a chuckle.

"Most definitely," she replied. "So how do you find yourself here tonight?"

His dark eyes glittered in the candlelight. "I intend to marry soon. One rarely finds a proper bride anywhere else."

"Oh," she whispered, heat infusing her cheeks. "Then I am doubly sorry that you ended up with me as a dance partner rather than my sister."

"I'm not," he replied quickly. "But tell me why you say that."

"She will be at many events this year. With my sister Emily newly wedded, it will be Diana's first season."

He quirked a brow, spinning her again. "Will your parents insist that you wait to marry until she's made a match?"

Cordelia's blood froze. This was a rather intimate conversation for a first dance. Why was that stranger so interested in her? She swallowed. Hopefully by the end of the night she'd find out. "I have no idea. I don't think they've considered the possibility, to be honest."

"And Lord Malicorn. Is he also a contender for your hand?"

Contender? "I don't...that is to say...I'm not entirely clear..." She ceased talking. Had Lord McKenzie noticed Chad's gaze upon them?

"I'll take that as a yes. Coupled with the fact that you danced with him twice and your stumbling answer, he must have expressed some interest."

Cordelia licked her lips, a nervous habit she often indulged in. She was not certain if she should

A single candle caught his notice in one of the windows above. Squinting, he caught sight of a nymph-like figure. Was that Cordelia? It certainly wasn't her mother. Too small. It could be one of her sisters?

He considered his options. He could stare and risk a passerby seeing him. He could toss a pebble at the window, and potentially alert someone besides Cordelia he was here. Would anyone else even recognize him in the dark?

He doubted it very much. Looking about the front garden beds, he found several small rocks that were about the right size. He lobbed one up and hit the siding of the house. "Bullocks," he muttered.

Picking up another, he tossed it again and hit the shutter next to the window. He was going to need more rocks.

Climbing back into the garden bed, he felt around with his hands, the dirt cool to the touch.

That's when he heard the distinct sound of the sash sliding open. "Who goes there?"

He was bent over, nearly under the privet but he'd recognize Cordelia's voice anywhere. "Corde? It's me."

She gasped. "Chad?"

Why did his name sound so good on her lips? "Yes, love. I need to talk with you."

There was a pause, in which he crawled out from under the hedge and stood. Looking up, he could see her dark figure half-hanging out the window. "Meet me at the garden gate in five minutes."

She withdrew back inside and he thought for a moment she wasn't going to answer. Then suddenly she was out again.

"But if we're caught, do you swear that you'll marry me?" she asked.

He stopped. There were worse fates. "Yes. I swear on my mother's grave."

She didn't answer right away, but he heard her intake of breath. "I believe you." Then she leaned back into the window, grabbing the sash to pull the glass back into place. "Go to the alley on the left. You can't miss the gate."

"Cordelia," he called, tugging at his coat. "I need you to help me—"

"I know," she answered. "I'll be right down."

How could she possibly know? Shaking his head, he started for the gate.

He found it easily enough but it was several minutes before Cordelia made her way down. He nearly missed her in the dark as she wore a long cloak with a hood. "Probably wise. Your outfit will help keep you from being discovered."

She paused on the path, lowering the hood. "That is one of the many advantages."

He quirked a brow. "What would the others be?"

Cordelia's fingers pressed to her cheeks. "It's quite warm."

Malice wanted to further question her. She was clearly embarrassed about something. It was in her tone, her hunched shoulders. But there were more pressing matters. "Thank you for meeting me."

She gave her head a small shake. "I shouldn't have come."

"Why?" His gut twisted.

A sliver of moonlight came out as she nibbled at her lip. "We could be caught. I don't relish marrying a man who was forced into the match."

He reached out and took her hand. "I know. You want a man to woo you."

She allowed him to pull her closer. "You make it sound silly."

"It isn't silly at all, wanting to feel loved. I understand it completely." Her cloak brushed his jacket and he wrapped a gentle arm about her back. "I'm sorry..." He stopped, realizing what he was about to say.

"What are you sorry for?" she asked, tilting her head back.

When she looked up at him like that, Malice

couldn't hold the words in. "I'm sorry that I didn't give you a better proposal. You deserve the best sort. I just, I'm not sure I'm capable. My heart is damaged, Cordelia." Maybe forever.

She reached up and touched his face. Not wearing any gloves, her velvet-soft fingertips made his heart beat wildly in his chest. "You don't have to explain to me."

"I do," he whispered and then he leaned down to place a light kiss on that lovely mouth. "I saw the way McKenzie was holding you tonight. He wants to lay claim."

She shuddered, pulling away. "That's absurd."

"It isn't." His tightened his hands on her waist. "Did he schedule another meeting?"

Cordelia swallowed, her delicate throat working. "He asked about my calling hours. But…" Her voice trailed off.

"I don't like him, Cordelia. There is something off there that I can't quite put my finger on. My name might be Malice but that man is cold."

She slid her fingers down to his neck, resting her palm against his skin. "But not you, you're warm."

Bending down again, he captured her lips in the dark night. "I'd keep you warm, yes. All through the long English winter."

She kissed him back, reaching up to hold him

CHAPTER EIGHT

MALICE SAT at the breakfast table of the Duke of Darlington, the Earl of Exmouth and the Viscount of Viceroy in attendance as well.

Not only did these men co-own the club, they were more like family than his own had ever been.

"I don't like that McKenzie fellow. That I can say for certain." He clenched his fork.

Vice, as they fondly liked to refer to the viscount, quirked a brow, his normally fair face looking rather mischievous. "You're not going to stab me with that utensil if I tell you the truth, are you?"

He narrowed his gaze. "I make no promises."

Exile cleared his throat, his powerful fist lightly banging the table. "There will be no stabbing."

Vice pushed his chair back, balancing on two

legs. "The truth is that you're good-old-fashioned jealous of the man." He gave him an angelic smile.

Darlington chuckled. "Jealousy is one emotion I can tolerate in this situation. It might prompt you to see reason."

Malice opened his mouth to tell Darlington to go to hell, but Vice answered first, the legs of his chair landing on the plush carpet with a decided thump. "You've gone bloody mad, Daring. Jealousy is the opposite of what Malice should be feeling. The man needs to remember this is a marriage of convenience. Now, if a mate tries to bed her after your wedding and then stick you with raising the pup, that's a whole different problem. But she's only one woman in a sea of choices. If McKenzie wants her then—"

Malice slammed his fist, still holding the fork, onto the table. He'd had enough of that sort of talk. "If you don't shut up, I'm going to take Exile out first just so that he can't stop me from killing you."

"If you scratch my table, you're replacing it," Darlington added, his voice even and light. "And I had the wood shipped from the Americas so it won't be cheap."

Exile chuckled, "Take me out. You've gone mad if you think you're big enough."

Malice drew in a deep breath. "McKenzie isn't

laying a hand on her now or in the future. I don't like him one bit and I just have a feeling that he'd bring Cordelia nothing but misery."

"I'm inclined to agree." Exile nodded as he scooped up a large bite of eggs. "The man is in gambling debt up to his eyeballs. Owes half the clubs in town. He's likely looking for a bride to bail him out of his troubles."

Malice sucked in a breath. Of course he was. He'd only asked Cordelia to dance after Diana had refused. The man wanted to wed the first purse that accepted him. "We have to stop him before he convinces Cordelia that he's a proper candidate for her hand."

"Are we stopping you too?" Daring asked leaning forward on his elbows. "You only want her to wed to make an heir and then shove her into the country. How is your offer any better than his?"

Damn Daring and his reason. His gut clenched. "I was honest, at least. I gave her the opportunity to refuse me on fair ground." If McKenzie realized how much Cordelia wished for romance than he might use that information to manipulate her into a match.

Somehow, he managed to squeeze the fork even tighter as he pushed the plate away. "You understand." He rubbed his neck, looking at each of the men. "She's been passed over as men have courted her sisters. It only takes one man to realize she wants to feel special and he'll be able to completely take advantage of her. By the time she realizes, it will be too late."

His words were met with silence.

Finally, Vice broke it. "If you ask me, it's already too late."

"It is not," he fired back, straightening. "We can protect her from making a mistake and ruining her future."

"I'm not talking about her." Vice crossed his arms. "I'm referring to you. It's too late for you, you've gone and developed feelings." He gave a shiver. "Christ, Jack made that joke at the club. Do you remember it? Careful, or you'll all catch feelings. Like it was a disease. Well it bloody may very well be contagious."

"Stop being ridiculous." Malice's own heart began thumping loudly in his chest. "I don't develop feelings. I can't. I swear my heart is so scarred that it couldn't feel if I tried."

"Dear God." Vice stood, his lip curling. "Are you talking about her healing your broken heart? This is bloody worse than I thought."

Daring gave a snort and then a laugh. "I think it's fantastic."

"I haven't caught feelings," he choked, rising as

bent down as she determinedly continued to knit her single long row.

McKenzie turned back to her, and reaching out his hand, brushed his thumb along the top of her cuff along her gloved hand. The touch was intimate and likely should have sparked excitement but she felt nothing. "That's very kind of you."

"I'm not being kind, Lady Cordelia. I'm being honest. You have your own charm. Tell me, can you see without the spectacles?"

What did that have to do with anything? She shifted in her seat as she fixed the spectacles. "Not particularly."

His smile slipped for a moment, before he put pulled the corners of his mouth back up. "Well, no matter. They hold their own charm."

Why did she get the impression he didn't mean those words? Not that they mattered. She leaned back, pulling her hand from his grasp. "I've always found vision to be preferable over blindness."

Her mother's needles ceased clicking and she made a definite tsking noise.

Cordelia's spine snapped straighter. "Tell me, Lord McKenzie, do you live in London most of the time?"

"Of course," he answered, relaxing back. "The country isn't the life for me."

Cordelia nodded as though she understood, though she didn't at all. She loved the country with quiet strolls and wide-open spaces and reflective time to think and write. "I see. What don't you like about it?"

He wrinkled his face in distaste. "What's a man to do but sit and think? Maybe walk, dreadfully boring."

She nodded again, thinking she must look ridiculous as her glasses slid down her nose. "And what of your life in London? What sorts of adventures do you partake in here?"

He pressed his lips together. "Fishing for information, are we?"

She shrugged. "Would you care to ask me a question in return? We're getting to know each other, are we not?" She didn't bother to mention with each sentence he uttered, she grew more certain, there was no future for them.

"We are and I would." He leaned forward and dropped his voice. "Tell me about that Marquess who looked rather possessive last night. Is he a serious candidate for your hand?"

Her stomach clenched as she thought about Chad. They'd kissed twice and he'd asked her to marry him. But she still wasn't entirely certain of the answer. "That depends, I suppose."

while at least he knew for sure he made her feel warm and desired. She'd said so herself.

Bounding up the steps, he hit the knocker on the door and was immediately seen in.

He heard voices coming from a sitting room to the right. He recognized Cordelia's light, high, tinkling voice immediately. When he heard the deep rumble of a man, he didn't have to guess who might already have arrived.

His chest tightened as he followed the butler toward the already open door. They were discussing him. He could hear himself being referenced. He supposed that was good. Even when not in the room, he was a topic of conversation; but still, Cordelia did not sound certain about him at all.

As the butler stepped in to announce him, he caught sight of his frowning little fairy. "That depends, I suppose."

His jaw clamped shut. Depends? Malice had kissed her senseless last night. How had she not told this man to leave immediately? "Depends on what?" he called, unable to help himself. He hated that she had told McKenzie that. Her words gave the man hope and alerted him to opportunity.

She stared back at him, her eyes unreadable behind her glasses. "That depends on you."

When he'd first met Cordelia, he'd thought her a malleable woman. She was quiet and often agreeable. But he realized now, behind her façade was a will made of iron. He rather liked it.

His body clenched in awareness and he stepped around the butler, foregoing the introduction. "Well, since I am part of this conversation, I'll answer Lord McKenzie. I am possessive because I intend to marry Lady Cordelia." He paused looking to the corner, "With Lord Winthrop's permission of course."

Lady Winthrop squeaked from the corner while Cordelia's cheeks flushed with color, making her look rather invigorated. Desire pulsed through him.

McKenzie stood, his fists clenching. "No one told me the lady was spoken for."

Cordelia stood too, her eyes darting between the two men. "Really, my lords. This isn't necessary."

"Do you consent to be my wife?" Malice asked her, stepping closer. If she agreed, he'd toss this upstart out by his ear. If she didn't, well, he'd toss him out anyhow but the man would have more cause to put up a fight.

He held his breath, realizing that he wanted her to say yes. He was invested now. He'd sift through his feelings and fears later but right now he wanted Cordelia to be his wife.

CHAPTER TEN

DAMN...MALICE'S jaw ached like bloody hell, not that he cared. He'd heard the crunch and now Cordelia lay limp in his arms.

That piece of shite, McKenzie, was gone and around him, three gaggling females crowded about, their noise so constant, he couldn't discern one voice from another. "Diana," he gritted out from between his teeth. "Get the doctor. Now."

He cradled Cordelia's head as he slowly rocked forward, shifting her weight so that he might sit with her in his lap. "Grace, is that your name?"

The blonde nodded. He was surprised how much she and Cordelia looked alike when Corde didn't have her glasses on. "Go to the kitchen and fetch anything cold." They spun and raced for the kitchen. "Lady Winthrop. Can you carefully take her arm and lift it over my head? I want to see what damage has been done."

"Oh dear," Lady Winthrop mumbled. "I'm not sure I can. I'll have to send for my husband."

Malice didn't want to wait that long. "You can do it. Where does she look injured?"

Lady Winthrop nibbled her lip as she leaned over him. He nearly choked because she looked exactly as Cordelia did. "Her hand is terribly swollen."

"All right. Grab her gently by the wrist and elbow and bring the arm over my head. Nice and easy and she won't feel a thing."

"Are you certain?"

Lady Winthrop's voice shook, but she did as he said and soon the hand was tucked between them. He could see that it was already swollen but the bones looked as though they were still in place. His shoulders slumped in relief.

Gingerly, he got to his knees and cradled her against his body as he slowly stood. He wanted to pepper her face with kisses to wake her. She'd been injured while keeping him safe. He couldn't quite define what that meant to him, but something inside him shifted. He'd known that he was attracted to her, that he even held some affection for her, but who had ever put themselves in harm's way to protect him?

"Lady Winthrop, shall I carry Cordelia to her room?"

"Oh, her room. Is it proper?" The other woman had both hands on her cheeks. "I mean, I suppose it's fine. She isn't even awake but—"

"Perhaps you can escort me. I don't know the way anyhow." He gave the woman an encouraging smile.

She nodded, her hands threading together. "Will she be all right?"

He gave her a quick nod of affirmation. "As far as I can see, it's a mild break. She'll be fine." His insides clenched. This had better be true because he'd only just found her and besides, she'd yet to reply to his offer of marriage.

Lady Winthrop reached out a trembling hand and touched Cordelia's forehead. "She's my kindest daughter. Would give every possession she had to make her sisters happy."

He'd seen that. Last night at the ball, she'd been completely willing to step aside to allow Diana a chance with McKenzie.

"Chad," she whispered, stirring a bit in his arms. "Is that you?"

"It's me, sweetheart," he replied, brushing his cheek to the top of her head.

"Are you all right?" she asked, tipping her head back to look up at him.

He looked down at her half open eyes. "I'm fine. Don't you worry about me. It's you we've got to mend."

"Your head…" she mumbled.

"It's not my first punch to the jaw. Likely won't be my last."

She shook her head. "No, no…the back. I tried to make sure it didn't hit the floor. I…" her voice tapered off as her eyes squinted to study him.

His insides clenched. She'd gotten injured deliberately to protect him. He'd suspected that, of course, but to hear her say it. "Thank you, Corde, for protecting me. Now shush while I take care of you. How is your hand?"

"It hurts," she answered, leaning her head into his chest. "A great deal."

"The doctor will be here soon."

She tilted her head back to look up at him again. "Did Lord McKenzie leave?"

Irritation sizzled down his spine. That man needed a serious beating. The sort that would remind him to be a gentleman and not go around throwing punches in a lady's company. "He did. But don't worry. I'll take care of him later."

"Don't bother." Cordelia closed her eyes and

tucked into his arm again. "He was upset because he knew he wasn't going to win against you."

That made him smile. He'd already offered for her hand and so he bent down and placed a soft kiss on her forehead. "That's kind of you to say, and I appreciate it a great deal, but I'm still teaching that man a lesson in the very near future."

"Oh do," Lady Winthrop sniffed. "We can say one thing for certain, however. I might have thought him a good candidate if not for today. His family has excellent bloodlines."

Cordelia gave an audible sigh and he pressed his lips together to keep from smiling. "Mother, bloodlines? Really?" Then she looked at him. "What did you mean when you said to him that you knew his motives?"

He frowned. "Just that I've heard he carries a great deal of debt at several clubs." He didn't mention his own establishment of course, but Cordelia's eyes widened.

"He's looking for a purse," she whispered. "No wonder he was so quick to switch from Diana to me."

Inwardly, he winced. He hated that she thought herself so unattractive. "You're jesting. You had two men brawling over you this afternoon."

He felt her smile against his chest. "The highlight

of my romantic attempts. I shall remember this always."

"As will I," he answered. If there had been any doubt in his mind about proposing, there wasn't any longer. How could he let a woman go who'd thrown herself bodily into his protection?

But then he grimaced. How was he going to give her the affection she deserved?

———

CORDELIA WOKE SLOWLY, as if from a deep sleep. Had she slept funny on her hand? It ached terribly.

Her eyes blinked open but the room was fuzzy. Were people talking? Someone brushed her cheek. "Are you awake, Cordelia?"

Chad. She blinked several more times, attempting to bring her gaze into focus. Was Chad in her bedroom?

Another hand slowly bent her hand and pain throbbed all down her arm. "It's a break to be certain but not a serious one. Won't even require setting," another voice said. "She'll need to rest for several days and keep the hand still."

Her eyes finally came into focus and so did her mind. McKenzie had hit Chad while Chad had been holding her up. She grimaced, certain he would not

speed your recovery and now you've a watch person. You'll be healed in no time."

"Chad," she closed her lips, mumbling around the edge of the cup. "I don't want to take it."

He clenched his teeth. "Does she really need to?"

The doctor gave a nod. "The mixture will help her sleep and sleep will encourage healing."

She let out a sigh and opened her mouth. "You'll stay?" For now, she'd focus on healing. Despite the fact they'd agreed to marry, she had the impression this conversation was far from over.

CHAPTER ELEVEN

CHAD SAT by Cordelia's bed, watching the gentle rise and fall of her chest as the early morning sun filtered in through her windows.

There had been a bit of activity when her father had finally arrived home at the Chase townhouse and learned that a man had taken up watch in his daughter's bedroom. He'd had to assure Lord Winthrop that he'd marry his daughter posthaste before the man calmed, which was not much of a promise on Malice's part. He'd intended to expedite the process anyhow. There were advantages to being a marquess and this happened to be one of them.

Another benefit was that Lady Winthrop supported the match wholeheartedly and had bodily placed herself between Malice and her inebriated husband. Malice had said little, allowing Cordelia's mother to do most of the talking.

He'd learned a thing or two about handling drunk men from his days running the club. He also recognized Winthrop as a frequent customer at his establishment. He was more than a little relieved the man hadn't recognized him. They wore masks at the club, of course. And they'd floated more than one rumor that they were actually pirates, rather than lords, but still. The small domino that covered his face surely allowed a more discerning customer to recognize his identity. Then again, most men were well into their cups by the time Malice began circulating the floor.

He ran a hand through his hair. He'd slept a little last night, but he was tired enough that even his scalp hurt.

Drawing in a long breath, he looked to his right. There sat an open book on Cordelia's desk.

Without thinking he picked it up and read the half-filled page. He smiled as he realized it was a fictional scene of their actual dance and their kiss from the night before. Flipping back several pages, he read through the story, grinning widely. He was clearly the hero of this tale, and McKenzie was just an annoying complication. He sat up straighter, his tiredness vanishing and his chest swelling with pride.

And not just because he was her love interest after all. The story was wonderful. The characters dancing off the page and capturing him. But perhaps that was because he was one of them.

He had a niggle of doubt about the ethics of what he was doing but he flipped to the front of the book and read another story. One where he surely wouldn't be featured.

From the first word, the story captured him. It was about an orphan girl, overlooked by everyone around her. Inside, his chest tightened for the child as the story unfolded before his eyes.

He looked at the sleeping woman on the bed. Cordelia was not only breathtaking, loving, and full of compassion, she was talented beyond measure. His breath caught in his chest.

Without intending to, he read the next story. In it, this time the main character was a boy, the son of an affluent family. But his mother perishes and his father... The air rushed from his lungs. His father was cruel. The boy hid in an ocean cave he'd found and one day ran away to the cave. He was eventually found and beaten. Then the boy determined to run away and find real love. A family that actually cared about him. A family that loved him.

always." Then she let out a long sigh and quieted.

He was certain she was talking in her sleep. Not uncommon for someone who'd taken laudanum. He didn't answer and she didn't ask again, relaxing back into the bed. His own exhausted eyes drifted closed.

They were going to marry. But he had to confess, after that story, he was less certain that he wanted to. Was he opening himself up too far? Was he destined to be rejected again?

———

CORDELIA WOKE to reality coming in bits and pieces. The first was the terrible ache in her hand, radiating through her arm. She winced and attempted to move, only to realize she was snug up against some large, warm object.

She snapped open her gaze to find Chad lying next to her. He was pressed against her with an arm over her torso and a leg across hers.

She had to confess, despite the pain, the position was incredibly comforting. She snuggled in a little closer and Chad's eyes flew open. "You're awake."

She nodded. "I am."

"How are you feeling?" He raised his hand and placed it on her forehead.

"Fine," she answered, the feel of his large hand pressed to her head wonderfully comfortable. "How are you. Did you sleep at all?"

He shrugged and then rolled away from her. Immediately, she grimaced from the loss of his heat, his solid protective flesh. "I did better once I was next to you." He stood and stretched. "Your hand? Does it hurt?"

"Terribly," she whispered. Then she caught sight of her book. "Oh no." She tried to sit up too but her hand twinged terribly.

"What's wrong?" He leaned back over her and part of Cordelia wanted to beg him to lay down next to her again.

"I…I can't write with my hand like this. I was just in the middle of a story."

His face shuttered. "That's unfortunate."

Something was off. Perhaps her mind was just muddled but despite waking up to his body draped over hers, he didn't seem like himself. "Do you find it strange that I write?"

He stopped, staring down at her. "No, when I think about it, I'm not surprised at all. You are very observant and articulate."

She nearly sighed with relief but held it in, giving him a smile instead. "Thank you." But her smile quickly fell. "I wonder when I shall be able to write again."

He reached down to brush something from the fabric of her coverlet. "How long have you been writing?"

"The last few years. Most of my stories are children's tales." She pointed at the book on the desk. That's when she realized the book was closed. Hadn't she left it open to the page she'd been working on? Her brain was still a bit fuzzy.

"Yes," he murmured. "I have to confess that I read one or two." He looked at the floor, his cheeks actually turning a bit red. "Please forgive me."

"Is that why you're acting so strange?" Then she gasped, "You didn't like them."

She'd never actually shared any of her stories with anyone before. Her sisters were featured too prominently and, she had to confess, sometimes they played the part of villain.

Plus, she'd never considered herself particularly good. "It's all right. I understand. We need never speak of it again and once we're married, I won't leave the book about." Then she started to sit up, struggling to right herself while holding her arm still.

"Cordelia," he said as he bent down. "Let me." He

slid his arms under her and slowly lifted her into a seated position.

His touch eased her tension. But once he had her seated, he pulled his arms out and moved away. Her nose wrinkled. She'd like to hold his hand at least.

He cleared his throat. "You needn't hide your work. I should have known you'd be a gifted writer."

There is was again. He studied the floor as he spoke. Was he lying? "That's kind of you to say. Thank you."

"I'm not being kind." He glanced at her again, and she could swear there was an accusation in the narrow-eyed gaze.

She cocked her head to one side, her tongue darting out to lick her parched lips. "I'm quite thirsty," she said.

Immediately, he turned to pour her water. He gently brought the cup to Cordelia's lips and gave her several sips. She grimaced as her head fell back on the pillow. Chad was here filling her every need and yet he seemed upset with her. Or her stories?

"Better?" he asked.

"Much." She looked at him again. "Which stories did you read?"

"The one you're currently writing," he answered, putting the pitcher back as he straightened the contents on a table. "And the first two in the book."

So he'd read *Orphan Kate* and *The Boy with No Family*. Her titles had gotten significantly better. She'd been meaning to change both of those. Her hands twisted in the blankets. Had he liked her stories?

Then he looked at her again, his face tense. "Are you angry with me for prying?"

She shook her head. "No. Though I've never let anyone read them before. But it's all right for you not to like them." She twisted her hands in the blankets. "I only ever wrote them for myself. They were a way for me to reimagine my problems with a happy ending. They give me hope, I suppose."

He stilled then. "You write about your problems? The one about the boy. Surely, that isn't about you."

She nodded. "It is. I ran away to a cave once when we were spending the summer in Dover. It took them two days to realize I was gone. I was quiet. When they realized it, well, they weren't too happy. My mother said I gave her a terrible fright and I got a good licking for my trouble. No one ever asked me what possessed me to do such a thing. I thought that being invisible meant that I was unloved. Now I understand that they care in their own way for me. But that I need a husband who really sees me. Do you see now why I insisted you not shunt me off to the country?"

This time he sat on the bed next to her. "I do." Then he drew in a shuddering breath. "In your writing, you have a real gift for expressing and touching the pain within. I honestly thought you might have told that story about me."

Now things were becoming clear. "Let's order some tea and then you can tell me about your childhood. It's time."

to what you will need from our marriage." If he was being honest with himself, she'd shown him what he needed. He hadn't wanted affection and love, but he'd found it and needed it more than ever.

"I've already told you what I'll need." He sat up then. "I need an heir. And I've agreed that I will not leave you in the country, we will remain together as a committed couple. A concession on my part considering my past."

Her eyes fluttered closed, her long lashes resting on her cheeks. "You'll need more than an heir. I do believe that you will need my affection. It's the only thing that heals wounds like you have."

She didn't open her eyes but he started to speak several times and then stopped again. Was she serious? Her solution was to give him more affection? Part of him rebelled. He'd only hurt her. But another deeper part cried that she was right. The only solution was to bask in the glow of her affection.

He'd have to work doubly hard to keep up some barriers between them. If he didn't, he'd only hurt her in the end, or even worse, wound their child, when he couldn't return the sentiment they so willingly gave.

———

THREE DAYS PASSED WITHOUT INCIDENT. More precisely, Cordelia reflected, not one single thing of any interest whatsoever had happened. She let out a loud sigh that no one heard, of course. She'd been in her room. Alone.

That wasn't entirely true. Her sisters had been in and out for several visits but they were busy and their stays were often brief.

Diana was acting strange to be certain, disappearing for large chunks of time, and Grace kept a full social calendar.

At least another letter had arrived from Emily. The couple was on their way home to explain their elopement. Relief flooded Cordelia at the knowledge their eldest sister was returning home. As she'd married an earl, her mother would most definitely forgive the offense and already planned to host another English ceremony to see the union recognized. Her father was furious but he'd come around. Her mother would see to that.

Cordelia picked at the covers and, finding them stifling, tossed them off and climbed gingerly from the bed. She was tired of laying around doing nothing.

The ache in her hand was slowly receding, which was nice, but she still couldn't use the blasted thing for much.

Crossing the room, she pulled the cord to call her maid. She desperately needed a bath and to dress in real clothing. And she needed to find people, or if everyone was occupied, lose herself in a story. She could read one, or have someone help her to write?

An hour later, she was dressed in a simple high-waisted gown of French cotton in a soft pink color. It was one of her favorite shades, bringing color to her face. The dress made her feel fresher even if her arm ached.

Picking up the quill with her left hand, she sat for an hour, not writing her story but making notes about the next several scenes. She knew the story was about her courtship with Chad but what she hadn't decided was whether or not the ending would mimic the truth. Despite her feelings, she doubted Chad would ever profess his undying love. Would her heroine get the happily ever after that Cordelia might never experience?

Her thoughts, along with the laborious task, soon sapped her of energy and she pushed back from the desk. All the same, she was satisfied with the results. She used the feather tip of the quill and brushed it along her cheek as she pictured Chad. He hadn't been to see her since he'd left the morning after her injury.

His absence did little to improve her mood. She

should be happy—she was engaged—but the truth was, she was far from secure in the knowledge. She'd meant what she'd said. She would try her best to heal his past.

But she needed to actually see him and spend time with him in order to do that. And his absence made her doubt his word. Would he change his mind and ship her off to the country to live alone after they were married? Perhaps, she'd made a mistake after all.

Rising again, she left her room and headed toward the family salon.

She could hear feminine voices floating down the hall and she stopped for just a moment to listen to her mother and sisters.

"I dare say, I can't believe how quickly this has all happened," Grace said, her voice rising higher. "A few days ago I didn't think Cordelia even liked the man."

Cordelia pressed her lips together to keep from making noise then covered her mouth with her hand. They were discussing her.

"What's not to like," her mother replied. "He's handsome in his own way and well-titled."

"Mother." Grace clicked her tongue. "There's more than a title to a good marriage."

"Thank you, Diana, for understanding that an apology is appropriate here. Just because I am quiet doesn't mean you can treat me like I don't exist."

"We're not doing that. You have your stories and—"

Cordelia stomped her foot, which made her arm jolt with pain that she ignored. "My hand is broken, mother. I can't write. And besides, I write the stories because they fill my time and in them, my family doesn't ignore me."

"That's not fair." Grace stepped forward. "You like to be by yourself."

"Not for days," Cordelia huffed. "Did he even ask about me? Where are the letters?"

"Letters?" Her mother crinkled her brow. "What do you mean?"

"What do I mean? How else did you do all that planning?" Her good hand, holding up her sore one, tightened on the skin.

"We didn't write, dear. He came here. It's where the breakfast will be after all."

Her eyes blurred with tears. "He was here? Today?"

"Just for a little while." Her mother took a few steps toward her. "We did most of the planning yesterday."

He'd been here multiple days? And he hadn't visited her or even sent a note? Was her marriage going to be exactly as her relationship with her family was? Did she really want that? The answer was no.

CHAPTER THIRTEEN

MALICE SAT in the seedy back room of their club with his head propped on his elbow as he allowed coins to drop from his hand one at a time. He wasn't sure when he'd decided he hated the club but somewhere during the past week his feelings had changed.

He didn't want to be here. Instead, he'd like to be curled against Cordelia's side, cradling her hurt arm. Pathetic.

Naturally, he'd stayed as far from her as he could. He fully intended to continue on with the wedding and he'd promised to keep her in London with him. Which meant he'd spend even more time here. He grimaced at the smoke-covered walls. When had this place become so dreadful?

"I swear, you are single-handedly creating an air

of gloom about the place." Bad, the Baron of Baderness, frowned around the cigar tucked between his teeth. "And that's coming from me."

Bad was a quiet and intense man, not that Malice cared. Except for right this moment when his friend insinuated that Malice was being morose. "I'm not making it gloomy. That is thanks to the damn cigar. Where did you get that thing? It stinks to high heaven and is blackening the walls."

Exile laughed as he stacked another pile of coins. "First it's the cigar smoke, then it's the drinking men. Next thing you know, we'll be losing yet another member of our little tribe."

"Bloody hell," Bad spit out between his teeth. "You're not falling for a Chase woman, are you?"

"Don't be so dramatic, it doesn't suit you." Malice grimaced over the table. The truth was, he began to wonder if he had fallen in love with her. The past three days without Cordelia had been...miserable. He'd moped about like a lovestruck lad with his first crush. But that couldn't be true. How could he have any heart left to give and what would he do when Cordelia realized he wasn't worth loving in return?

Bad smacked the table. "Thank God. I thought you'd been laid low by a clumsy, four-eyed blue-stocking who isn't even that pret—"

He surged to his feet in a second, his chair hitting

the floor with a thud that echoed about the small room. "Finish that sentence and I'll hit you so hard that you won't wake for a fortnight."

Bad tipped his chair back, taking a long pull from his cigar before he plucked the smoking stick from his mouth. "I thought insults might draw out the truth. You've fallen in love."

Malice's chest was still puffed out and he drew back his chin. "How I feel has little regard in the matter. I'm marrying her."

"When will you take her to the country?" Exile asked, moving a neat stack of coins next to the others.

He hesitated, dropping his arms a bit. "I'm not taking her at all. She's staying here with me. We made a deal."

Exile raised a brow. "So you are in love then."

"I'm not." He cut his hand through the air. "I can't be. I'm not capable of the emotion and even if I was, I wouldn't want to feel it. It's nothing but trouble. A hinderance that leaves you open for hurt."

Exile nodded. "I agree. I feel the same."

Bad shrugged, bringing his cigar back to his lips. "We are all of the same mind, but I think you might be of a different heart. You can't marry her, live with her every day, and not develop an attachment. It's impossible. You either have to resign yourself to emotional involvement, marry her and send her away, or not marry her at all."

Malice grimaced as he reached down to pick up his chair and then sat back down in the seat. "I'm afraid you're right about that."

Exile started a new stack. "You can't back out of the wedding. She'd be ruined, which is exactly what we're trying to avoid. Out of sheer spite, she might very well share that we are owners of the club."

Malice ran his hands through his hair. "She wouldn't accept the proposal without a promise that she stay in London."

Bad coughed. "And you conceded? Why?"

Malice scrubbed his face. He knew why. He loved her. He bent his head, staring at the floor. When had this happened and how had he not realized. He wanted nothing more than to stay by Cordelia's side forever. "This other fellow, Lord McKenzie, was sniffing about her. He only wants her dowry and I—"

"McKenzie?" Bad growled. "Why didn't you say so?"

"What do you mean?" Malice sat up straight as an arrow.

"He's in my boxing club. Dirty fellow, never fights fair. He gambles here too. A great deal. In fact, he owes us a sizable debt." Bad leaned forward, his elbows on the table. "But worst of all, I've seen him on several occasions with the Countess of Abernath on his arm."

"The Countess of Abernath?" His heart thudded in his chest. "She was supposed to be at the ball the other night."

"So?" Exile sat straighter. "You were with Cordelia and Diana. The countess never came."

"Yes, but McKenzie did. And he made his was directly to Diana and Cordelia. When Diana refused his dance, he immediately went to Cordelia and he's been hanging about her ever since." His hands shook. "It can't be a coincidence that the Countess of Abernath's lover is now sniffing about a Chase girl."

"Bloody hell, it can't." Exile was on his feet too. "We need to warn the girls."

But Malice didn't answer. He was already shrugging on his coat as he sprinted for the door. He needed to see Cordelia right this moment. He just wanted to know she was safe.

———

CORDELIA HAD SAT for hours in her room alone. This time, her mother and both of her sisters had attempted to visit but she'd sent them away. She'd said too much. Or not enough. She wasn't certain.

Perhaps she was to blame. They'd pay her more mind if she were funnier, or more sociable.

That was likely why Chad had stayed away. He'd decided she'd make a suitable wife and that's what she would always be to him. Nothing more. Or perhaps, now that she'd agreed to marry him, he was no longer interested in making her feel special. Either way, she was worried she'd made a terrible mistake.

A tear trickled down her cheek and she swiped it away. They only fogged up her glasses. She couldn't do it. She couldn't marry a man who barely noticed her. His indifference would crush her.

Another knock sounded at the door. "Please. I don't want visitors."

"Very well, my lady," the butler answered. "Should I tell Lord McKenzie to come back another time?"

"Lord McKenzie?" She sat straighter. "Here now?"

"Yes, my lady," the butler replied. "Though it's nearly five, it is technically still your calling hours. Should I fetch Mary to sit with you or should I ask Lord McKenzie to return another time?"

She licked her lips, standing. She likely shouldn't see him after the way he'd acted. "I don't think it's wise."

"Very well, my lady. Can I at least deliver his gift to you?"

"Gift?" she asked, crossing the room. "What gift?" Then she opened the door. Mr. Bradley didn't bother to answer as he handed her a large bouquet of white orchids. "He sends his sincerest apologies."

"He shouldn't be giving me gifts." But heat filled her cheeks. No man had ever attempted to give her a trinket or flower. It was a promise of sorts and her stomach flopped at the idea of a man being so bold.

"I misspoke. He said it wasn't a gift and shouldn't be taken as such but an apology for his behavior. He wishes to know that you are well after your fall."

She set the flowers on the table and turned back to Mr. Bradley. "I suppose I can see him for a bit to allow him to apologize. Fetch Mary, please, and request tea and biscuits."

"Very good, Lady Cordelia." He nodded as he turned to go do as she'd requested.

She made her way down the sitting room, relieved to find none of her family there. Her cousin, Mary, however, had already stationed herself in the corner. Mary was a lovely woman with dark hair and eyes. Not the first time, Cordelia wondered why she'd never married. "Good evening, Mary."

"Cordelia." The other woman smiled back with a wink. "You won't even know I'm here."

She gave Mary a nod as she took a seat on the settee. Her movements were ginger to say the least. Her arm had been wrapped in strips of cloth and a sling had been formed to keep the hand from moving but it still ached a bit this time of day.

Not two minutes later, the door opened again and the butler entered with McKenzie. He immediately held out his hands. "Is that a sling? I am so sorry. Please don't get up." He held out his hands as he crossed the room to her. "I am a complete boar. Say that you'll forgive me."

She pressed her lips together, remaining in her seat. What had seemed like a reasonable idea in her room, suddenly felt off. Wrong. She'd been desperate for a bit of company that didn't feel strained, but McKenzie should not have been the answer. If anything, he was far meaner than her family or Chad. "Of course I can forgive you. I hope you'll forgive me, I can only visit for a short time. I find I have very little energy."

He waved. "Certainly. I understand completely."

The butler gave a quick bow and turned to go just as the tea service arrived. The maid set it on the table next to the settee. Cordelia grimaced as she realized she'd have to rise. When she'd ordered the drink, she'd forgotten she'd need to serve it to a guest. It was going to be challenging with one hand.

"How delightful." McKenzie beamed. "I was going to request tea. Long day. So thoughtful for you to have ordered it already."

"Were you?" She crinkled her brow, trying to decide why this entire visit seemed strange. Placing her good hand on the seat, she started to push up when he held out his hands. "Please allow me. You shouldn't get up on my account."

He stood at the table, arranging cups and pouring liquid. Cordelia wasn't certain she'd ever seen a man serve tea before and her eyes narrowed. "Are you certain I can't help you?"

"You could help me by looking away." He turned back to her giving her a large smile that showed all his teeth. "I feel odd. Not that I'm not happy to help, but I'm afraid this doesn't come naturally to me."

Cordelia nodded and looked across the room. Something was wrong with this meeting. He was too smiley, too helpful. Did he really feel that guilty or did he want to change her mind about marrying Chad?

"Here you go." McKenzie said but his voice was further away.

Cordelia turned her head to see that he'd served Mary a cup of tea. The other woman crinkled her brow in confusion as she accepted the cup.

Cordelia opened her mouth to ask what he was

doing, but then closed it again. She didn't want Mary to feel badly for accepting the cup. "Lord McKenzie," she asked instead. "Are you feeling all right?"

"I'm grand." There it was again. That toothy smile. But he set a cup of tea down on the table in front of her holding a second in one his large hand. "I'm thrilled you agreed to see me after what happened. I have to confess that I can be a bit of a jealous man. But I went too far and I'm so glad to have this opportunity."

She nibbled at her lip, deciding this was an even larger mistake than she'd first supposed. She didn't want to spark any negative behavior by telling him that she'd accepted Chad's offer and she doubted McKenzie could provide much clarity on whether or not she should retract from the match. Instead of saying anything, she took a sip of her tea.

Immediately, she realized it tasted funny. Sweeter than normal. She set the cup down. "Don't drink that, my lord. Something's wrong with it."

His face went pale. "What do you mean?"

Her own eyes narrowed. "It tastes odd. I'll have to ask the cook what…" Her voice tapered off as she tried to rise but her head swam. She sat back down instead. "Mary. Did you taste anything off?"

Cordelia turned to look back at Mary. The other woman was slumped over in her chair. "Mary!"

Her own voice made her head pulse and she brought her good hand up to press against her forehead. "Lord McKenzie, I don't feel well."

She closed her eyes to try and clear the cobwebs but jolted them open again when large hands circled her shoulders. Her vision was cloudy. "I know you don't, but don't worry. You'll be asleep very soon."

"Asleep?" she asked but her voice came out funny. Like her tongue was too large for her mouth.

She tried to clear her mind, but the harder she worked the worse it became and suddenly the world went black.

CHAPTER FOURTEEN

MALICE JOGGED up the steps to the Chase townhouse as the sun dipped lower in the sky, his stomach sinking with the setting sun. His fist clenched as he raised a hand to bang the knocker on the front door. Somehow, he just needed to see Cordelia and know for certain she was safe.

Bloody bullocks, he was failing her already. He'd stayed away to protect her. His insides twisted. That wasn't true. He'd stayed away to protect himself. And in doing so he'd put her in danger.

He took a deep breath. He didn't know that. In fact, he was likely letting his worries run away with him. Someone would answer the door soon and show him upstairs. She'd be lying in bed and likely miffed that he hadn't been to visit her in person for three days.

He smiled, relaxing a bit. He'd have to beg for her forgiveness. He was fine with that. Then, he'd tell her how he felt. Which was to say, he'd tell her that he loved her, was in love with her and...he paused. What was taking so long?

He raised his hand and knocked again. Louder.

After several more seconds he heard hurried footsteps crossing the foyer and then the door jolted open. The butler looking pale and shaken stood before him. "My lord," he cried the moment he saw him. "Thank goodness it's you."

"It's me," he answered stepping inside. "Why are we giving thanks for that?" But the sinking feeling he'd had all day returned. He pulled his shoulders straighter as though bracing himself. "What's happened?"

The man grew more pale. "Come with me and I'll explain." Then he turned and started up the stairs. "Lady Cordelia had a visitor," he said over his shoulder as they walked.

"Who?" He quickened his pace, not wanting to miss a word.

"Lord McKenzie," the butler answered, stopping on the steps. "It was during calling hours. They were chaperoned."

Malice placed his hand on the man's back giving him a small push forward to keep him going. He needed to get upstairs and see Cordelia. "I'm sure it was all very proper. What's happened. Is she all right?"

"Mary's still asleep so I'm not entirely sure what's happened, and Lady Winthrop has fainted, and Lady Diana has sent a servant to find her father, but…"

His gut knotted in fear as he drew up to his full height. "Where is Cordelia?" Anger and fear were making his voice rise louder.

The man made it to the top of the stairs and stopped again, turning to face him. He swayed on his feet. "That's just it, my lord. We don't know. She's gone."

"Gone?" Malice stopped too, gripping the banister so tightly, he thought it might break. "What do you mean she's gone?"

The other man swallowed. "Well. I left her and Mary in the sitting room with Lord McKenzie. When I returned, Mary was laying on the floor. Lord McKenzie and Lady Cordelia had disappeared."

"Where are they?" He knew he was being obtuse. But the idea that Cordelia could be anywhere in London or even out of the city by now made his head spin. "How long ago did you discover this?"

"Just an hour ago, my lord." The man took several shallow breaths. "What are we going to do?"

He didn't know for certain and he scrubbed a

hand along the back of his neck. He wanted to curl into a ball and cry like he hadn't since the age of five when his nanny had left. Instead, he twisted his neck, giving it a crack. "We're going to find her and then we're going to kill Lord McKenzie." He let go of the banister and started down the hall. "Show me the sitting room."

"Yes, my lord." The butler came to life, moving down the hall. "How did you know to come here?"

He shook his head. "It was just a feeling." It wasn't any old feeling. It was the most powerful emotion he'd ever experienced. And now that he had found love for the first time in adult life, he was not losing Corde. She belonged to him now and forever and he needed to find her.

They rounded a corner and he stepped into the sitting room. Diana paced near the window, her hands clasped. The moment she saw him, she stopped pacing. "Thank goodness." She tossed her hands in the air.

He didn't say a word as he picked up an abandoned teacup and sniffed. "Opium," he said, his voice ruff. He'd recognize that sweet scent anywhere. No wonder Mary was a puddle on the floor.

"Opium?" Diana crossed over to him. "You're sure?"

He squeezed his eyes shut. Cordelia had been

drugged and now she could be anywhere. "What do we know?" He scrubbed his face. "We know she's asleep and that she could remain that way for hours. We know she's with McKenzie, or she was, and we know…" He hesitated, opening his eyes to look at Diana. He thought back to her comments about Lady Abernath wanting revenge. "We know that McKenzie and Lady Abernath are in a relationship."

Diana gasped, her hand covering her mouth. "Where would they take her?"

He shook his head. "That's what I don't know. But I know someone who might." He turned toward the door. "I'll send a missive as soon as I know anything."

"I'm coming with you." She straightened and began to follow.

"No," he said as he turned back to her. "Your reputation."

Diana pulled herself taller. "I don't care about that."

Malice paused. He didn't have much time but he appreciated what Diana wanted to do. "You'll slow me down. I'll be faster on horse on my own."

Her shoulders sagged a little. "I have to help her." A tear slid down Diana's cheek. "We take her for granted sometimes. She gives so much and asks so little."

He reached out and patted her shoulder. "I'll bring her back to you and then you can apologize in person. Now take care of your mother and tell your father what's happened. He needs to report McKenzie to the Bow Street Runners so that we have more men looking for them. Do you understand?"

Diana gave a tight nod. "Of course."

Malice turned toward the door and made his way down the hall and to the steps. As he passed under the ceiling painted with cherubs, he said a silent prayer that he was able to keep his promise to Diana. If he lost Cordelia now... He refused to finish the thought. He'd find her. For all their sakes, he had to get Cordelia back.

———

CORDELIA WOKE IN A DARK ROOM. The bedding was comfortable enough and the bed was large and quite fluffy, but the room smelled wrong. This wasn't her bed. Her head pounded and her mouth was pasty with thirst. "Hello," she called.

"You're awake," a voice called out of the darkness. "I was beginning to wonder if you'd sleep all night."

Cordelia scrunched her brow. The feminine voice was oddly familiar, high and cool in its tones;

it made her shiver even under the covers. "I'm quite thirsty."

"Oh yes, I can imagine so. You'll need food very soon too."

Cordelia heard the sound of metal scraping wood` and the fire jumped to life, casting shadows all about the room as it faintly illuminated the interior. She squinted her eyes, a statuesque figure standing next to the hearth. "What happened?"

The woman turned away from the flames and moved toward her to the table next to the bed. She lifted a pitcher and poured a glass of water. "You don't remember Lord McKenzie's visit?"

She raised a hand to her head. Vague memories of drinking very sweet tea came to mind. "What was in the tea?"

"Oh, I didn't ask that." The woman bent down with a glass of water in hand. "The less I know the better." Lady Abernath's face came into view and Cordelia gasped, recoiling on the bed. Some of the fog lifted from her brain but her head throbbed terribly.

"But if I were to guess by the way you were talking in your sleep, I'd say opium of some sort." She pushed the glass closer. "Now drink. You need your strength."

Cordelia swallowed, her lips sticking together.

Her mouth tasted like she'd eaten wood but after what had happened, she didn't think she should drink something offered by Lady Abernath. "I've changed my mind."

The other woman sighed and then brought the glass to her lips, taking a long swallow. "It's fine. I can assure you."

Cordelia stared at the liquid. It must be all right and she was unbelievably thirsty. She took the glass and brought it to her lips, taking a small sniff. The liquid smelled fine. Then tipping the glass, she took a small sip and then another. It slid down her throat, cool and refreshing, dulling the pain in her head.

"Better?" Lady Abernath crossed the room and pulled a cord. "Let's get a snack too. I'm terribly peckish after staying up all night."

Cordelia blinked. What exactly was happening here? Had she been stolen out of her home for a sleepover? Lady Abernath was acting as though they were friends. She clamped the blanket tighter to her body. "Why am I here?"

Lad Abernath pulled the cord. "Drink more water. You'll need it."

Cordelia stared at the other woman for a moment before she obeyed. With every sip, her headache lessoned. She didn't ask again, assuming she'd find out soon enough.

Lady Abernath gave instructions to a servant to prepare a tray and then returned to Cordelia's bed. Settling herself in a chair next to Corde, she leaned back, folding her hands over her knee. "You're here because I need your help."

"Help?" Cordelia struggled to sit up straighter. Between her arm, her head, and the glass of water, she made quite a mash of it. "You've abducted me and now you want my help?"

"I didn't abduct you. Lord McKenzie has that honor. I simply want to strike a bargain."

Cordelia gripped the glass tighter. "What sort of bargain?"

"It's simple enough. You want to return to your family, preferably without anyone realizing you were ever gone." Lady Abernath gave her a large smile that curled her lips, but nothing else on her face moved. Her eyes didn't crinkle, her cheeks didn't plump. It was the coldest smile Cordelia had ever seen. "I want all of England to know that the Duke of Darlington isn't the wholesome picture he presents to the world."

Cordelia drew in a sharp breath. She was beginning to understand "You want me to out Daring as the owner of the Den of Sins?"

Lady Abernath gave a small clap. "What a clever girl you are."

Cordelia shook her head. Lady Abernath was playing nice but this woman had most certainly orchestrated this entire event. "And if I refuse? Do I stay here as your guest?"

"Oh no. Certainly not," Lady Abernath gave a high trill of laughter. "But, I will make certain that all of London hears that you spent the night with Lord McKenzie. And as he is on a boat headed for France, he won't be available to save you from your fate."

"A boat to France?" Why on earth would the man agree to that?

Lady Abernath twirled her hand in the air. "Afraid so. He's carrying an amazing amount of gambling debt. He's got a real problem, I'd say. I gave him enough to help him live comfortably in another country but not enough that he could pay all his debts and remain here. It was a beneficial arrangement for both of us. He needed money to leave and I needed a means to an end."

Cordelia's stomach tightened. Lady Abernath had paid McKenzie to steal her away and now no one knew where she was or even that she was safe. How was she going to get out of this mess?

CHAPTER FIFTEEN

MALICE BURST into the back room of the club, his breath coming in short gasps. He needed to speak with Bad. His friend might know where McKenzie was, or at the very least, how to find the fiend who'd taken Cordelia.

But it wasn't Bad who sat in the back room but golden-haired Vice. "What's got you all aflutter?"

"Where's Bad?" he bit out, stopping just in front of the man. "I need him now."

Vice grimaced, rising up from his chair. "Exile. Malice needs Bad. It's an emergency."

"On it," Exile called from the hallway between the back room and the club itself.

Malice relaxed a bit as he drew in a breath. His friends made this easier. "I need Daring too. Can you fetch him for me?"

"Of course. What should I tell him has happened?" Vice was already shrugging on his coat.

"McKenzie has taken Cordelia." The words stuck in his throat, making the inside of his mouth feel swollen and raw.

Vice stopped, turning to stare at him. "What?"

"It's true. Now go. I'll need all of you to help me get her back."

Vice gave a quick jerk of his chin and then sprinted for the door. "I need a hack now!"

Exile came back in the room. "Bad will be here in just a moment. Did I hear you say that Cordelia has been stolen away by McKenzie?"

He nodded. "Yes. If I were to guess, he's taken her to Lady Abernath but I can't know for certain."

"I'd guess you were correct," Bad said from the doorway, pulling his domino from his face. Then he pointed down the hall. "If he were still with Cordelia then he couldn't be here."

A jolt of energy zinged down his spine. "He's here. Now?" He jumped toward the door, intent upon murdering the man at the table where he sat.

Both Exile and Bad blocked his way. "You can't kill him yet," Exile said close to his ear.

"I agree," Bad replied. "We need a plan."

Malice drew in several deep breaths. "Does the plan involve beating the piss out of McKenzie?"

"Absolutely." He snapped the domino back in place. "But let's get him in the back room first."

"How are you going to do that?" Malice asked.

"He's a degenerate gambler. I'm going to offer him a high stakes game in our private room. He's throwing immense amounts of coin around this evening."

That made Malice's gut clench. "I thought you said he was in debt up to his ears."

"He is." Bad shrugged. "But he got money from somewhere."

"Cordelia," Malice grit out. "Do you think Lady Abernath paid him?"

Bad gave him a one-sided grin. "Let's ask him, shall we?"

"Fantastic idea," Exile answered. "We'll sit at the table with our backs to the door so he thinks we're also here for the game. When you come in behind him, be sure to close the lock."

Malice slapped Exile on the back. "Good thinking." Then he hit him again. "I hope never to be on your bad side."

Exile winked. "I'm a kitten compared with you."

They crossed over to the table. Sitting in the chair and waiting was a small form of torture and minutes felt like hours as Malice flexed his fingers trying to remain calm. Finally, feet shuffled down the hall and the door clicked closed.

"My lord." Bad had a natural cockney accent that he broke out on the gaming floor. It helped maintain their secret and keep up the story that they were working men. As a result, Bad was often the man who monitored the tables and kept the peace. "Have a seat right next to that big fellow."

"Don't mind if I do," McKenzie answered, his voice chipper but slurred. "What a night. I should warn you gentlemen that fortune is on my side this evening." And he whistled as he sat.

Malice looked over at him, cracking his neck. "Is it really?"

McKenzie's eyes slowly focused on his face. It took several seconds before he started and tried to jump from his chair but Bad was already behind him and pushed him back into the seat.

"Don't move," Bad growled.

Malice stood. "This can go one of two ways. You can begin talking and we can have a nice conversation. Or you can resist, in which case I will enjoy breaking each of your limbs."

McKenzie swallowed. "Lady Cordelia is at the Countess of Abernath's townhouse. Or she was when I dropped her there at six."

Malice gave a curt nod. "Why did you take her?"

"Cristina…that is to say the countess…gave me money to leave the country. I've a boat to catch in a few hours."

Anger ripped at his nerves. The man was going to run from his debt. "You were never going to marry her, were you?"

McKenzie held up his hands. "I was. Until it was clear that you were going to best me. I need the funds. If I don't leave, I'll go to prison."

Malice's growl sliced the air. Had he just felt a glimmer of sympathy for this complete animal? His name was Malice, for feck's sake. He didn't feel anything for anyone.

Except for Cordelia. And now, he couldn't help but think about what she would do in this situation. "What time is your boat?"

McKenzie swallowed. "It sails with the tide at six this morning."

Malice looked at Exile. "Keep him here. I'll let you know if I find Cordelia. If I do and she's unharmed, see him to the boat."

"She will be," McKenzie held up his hands. "Cristina doesn't want to hurt her. She wants her to help in some nefarious plot."

"What plot?" Malice asked leaning closer.

McKenzie shook his head. "I don't know. She didn't say and I didn't ask. I assumed the less I knew, the better. Frankly, there have been a few times that I've questioned her sanity. She seems to lose herself somewhere in the past."

Malice straightened. He believed the man. Mostly because if Lady Abernath had told McKenzie that she wanted to out the owners of the Den of Sins, he wouldn't have arrived at this very club. "Why did you come here tonight?"

McKenzie looked down at his hands. "I thought I could increase my money before I left and this club has the highest stakes games in all of London."

Malice let out a snort of disgust. "Your problems will follow you wherever you go." Then he straightened. McKenzie wasn't the only man allowing his past to ruin his future. Malice had been doing the same. But not any longer. It was time to rescue the woman he loved. "Is your carriage outside?"

"Yes," McKenzie answered, his brow drawing together. "Why?"

"Give me your cloak."

"But," McKenzie covered the clasp with his hand. "I need this—"

Malice raised his hand and brought it down hard on McKenzie's face. He should have punched the piece of shit. He blamed Cordelia, she was making him soft. He'd have to kiss her over and over as her punishment. "Give it to me now. If she isn't there, you won't be needing it because you'll be at the bottom of the Thames."

With a trembling hand, the other man unclasped the wool garment and handed it to Malice. "She'll be there."

He grabbed the garment and then the collar of McKenzie's shirt, pulling the man half out of the chair as he leaned down in his face. "How do you enter the Countess's house? And remember…your life depends on Cordelia's safe return."

"I always come through the kitchen. Never the front door."

The outside door slammed open and Daring stood, filling the doorway with his dark glower. "What did I miss?"

Malice looked at his friend, dropping McKenzie back in his chair. "I'll catch you up on the way. We are headed to Lady Abernath's house to rescue Cordelia."

———

CORDELIA SAT in the bed slowly chewing a piece of cheese while the countess spread jam on a cracker and then popped it into her mouth. Her stomach turned. She should not, under any circumstances, be breaking bread with this woman. But then again, she needed her strength. Whatever they'd given her had made her sick to her stomach and the food was helping.

"Better?" Lady Abernath gave her another of those cold smiles. The sort that set Cordelia's teeth on edge.

"Yes, thank you, my lady." What was she doing? Her mother had drilled manners into her, but did she really need to thank her captor for a bit of cheese?

"Call me Cristina," she said as she picked up a cube of cheese. "McKenzie was right. You are very sweet. Too nice to be mixed up in this."

She opened her mouth but closed it again. She was tempted to ask, if they held her in such high regard why had they stolen her from her home, but it was likely a useless question. "And yet, here we are."

The smile slipped. "So, my dear, the sun will come up very soon. We could have you back in your bed before anyone in society is the wiser. All you have to do is agree to attend a party tomorrow night. At it, you'll tell everyone with an ear for gossip that you heard the Duke of Daring and the Earl of Effington secretly own and run London's most notorious gaming hell."

Cordelia nibbled her lip. "Can I ask you a question? How does that information hurt them? I'm not sure I understand."

Cristina nodded. "They've built the club by pretending to be pirates or thieves or something. Meanwhile they operate in society as if they have sterling reputations. They should suffer the way a woman would."

Cordelia rubbed her chin. "I'm inclined to agree that society is unfair to women." She didn't add that she doubted it would hurt the men that much. Did their livelihoods depend on the club's revenue?

And more importantly, what would happen if she refused the countess's offer? Or if she agreed and then didn't follow through? Or if…

"I see your little brain turning." Cristina leaned forward. "Did you know that they threatened me? Said they would have men claim to be my lovers and go to my husband?"

Cordelia suspected that the men really had been her lovers. "I'm sorry?"

Cristina nodded. "I only married the Earl of Abernath because Darlington left me for ruin. The man is cruel and repulsive." She gave a shiver then leaned forward. "He's taught me how to really hurt another person. Physically." Then Cristina reached out and took her hand. Pulling it toward her Cordelia tried to pull her arm back, but she was still so weak and the countess's grip was tight. Reaching for the candle, she dripped a large spot of burning hot wax on Cordelia's skin. Without meaning too, Cordelia let out a scream, the burn sending shivers up her arm as the pain amplified.

Quickly, Cristina let the arm go again and righted the candle. "I'm a nice person, Corde."

How did the other woman know her nickname? "But I've learned a great deal about you and your habits. Cross me and I will find you. And this was just a taste of what I will do to you."

Cordelia hugged her arm to her chest as the burning pain radiated along her skin. "And if I don't agree?"

The countess gave her that toothy smile as she leaned closer. "Then we'll have to convince you with some more wax." The other woman reached for her arm again and without meaning to, Cordelia let out another scream.

CHAPTER SIXTEEN

MALICE FLEXED his arms trying to remain calm as the carriage rumbled down the street. Inside, however, he was a frantic ball of nerves. He wanted his woman back and he wanted to make the countess pay.

"I can't believe she would go to this length." Daring shook his head. "I knew Cristina was deep down dark, but I didn't think she'd take innocent girls."

Malice squeezed his eyes shut. Apprehension curled in his stomach, spreading a nauseating sensation through his body. "Will the countess hurt Cordelia?"

Daring sighed, staring at the ceiling. "I don't know. I thought I knew her but I was proven wrong a long time ago."

"What happened between you?" Malice wasn't sure why he asked other than he needed something to pass the time and, perhaps if he understood the woman better, he'd better be able to fight her.

"I was courting her. Our relationship, at least the physical part, progressed. She was rather adventurous and I found it exciting." Daring looked out the window into the dark night. "When she became pregnant, I offered for her hand."

Malice nodded. He'd known most of this already. "How did it end?"

"I found her in bed with another man." Daring scrubbed his face. "I never learned who he was and I don't care. At the time I did, but now I realize that bloke did me a favor. I ended it with her and never looked back. She married Abernath a month later."

"And the child?" Malice asked.

Daring shrugged. "She lost the baby."

Malice scratched his chin. "By all accounts, you should be angry with her. Why does she hate you so much?"

Daring shook his head. "I honestly don't know. Looking back, I wasn't sure she ever even liked me. She seemed to hate me at times, and not just me. She didn't like men in general." He scrubbed his face with his hands. "She sent me several letters. In one of them, she accused me of ruining her future. Like I was to blame for ending our engagement. I suppose I was but…"

Malice let out a long breath. "She doesn't want to take accountability for her own actions." That made his gut tighten. A person like that was dangerous.

"Try not to worry." Daring looked over at him. The sun was just beginning to brighten the sky. "She must want Cordelia for a reason and it isn't just to hurt. How would that make me pay for my supposed sins?"

Malice scratched his head. "Why would she want Cordelia?"

Daring frowned. "I have no idea. Unless she thinks that Cordelia could ruin me?"

Malice's eyes widened. Of course. "She wants Cordelia to share what she knows about the club." Then he paused. "But why doesn't she share that herself?"

Daring shrugged. "She doesn't have a lot of sway left in society. She likely thinks a woman as pure as Cordelia could do far more damage."

The carriage began to slow. His insides contracted as he stood, opening the door before the carriage had even stopped. "I'm going to go in and pretend to be McKenzie. Follow in a few minutes and have your pistols ready."

Daring gave a terse nod. "Be safe."

"My safety isn't that important. But if something happens to me, see that Cordelia is married. To a nice man who reads her poetry and captures stars for her." Then he jumped from the carriage, making his way down the alley.

Daring stuck his head out the door. "So the opposite of you then?"

Malice bit back a smile. He likely was all wrong for Cordelia. But she had his heart now and he'd tell her come hell or high water. Hell, he'd die just to have the chance.

He made his way through the back gate and followed a path to a door at the back of the house. Entering by the kitchen, he heard one of the servants call out. "Hurry, she requested that tray five minutes ago."

Malice pulled the cloak tighter about this face. A servant came rushing from the kitchen and practically sprinted toward the back staircase. Only the mistress of the house could inspire that sort of fear and so he followed being careful to stay far enough back that he wouldn't be seen.

The servant went up two flights and disappeared in the third. Damn, maybe he'd left too much space because by the time he made it up the stairs, all the doors were closed. How would he figure out which room the woman had gone in? At the end of the hall were some curtains, he worked his way to the other end, and hid himself behind them. The window overlooked the street. Any more light outside and someone could look up and notice him standing in the window, but at least the fabric hid him from the hall.

Carefully, he peeked out of the one side and watched as the servant left from the third door on the right.

He let out a breath. He was assuming that was the countess's chamber but how to make certain? And from there, how would he find Cordelia?

He crept out from behind the curtains and slowly made his way down the hall, listening for any sound of voices or any other clue as to the occupants in the room. All was quiet as he reached the door. Slowly, ever so quietly, he turned the knob. When the latch finally gave way, he pushed the door the tiniest bit open. Then leaned over to peek inside, holding his breath. Was Cordelia here? His answer came not a second later as a blood curdling scream pierced his eardrums. Without another thought, he threw open the door.

———

CORDELIA SAT ON THE BED, her eyes wide as she

watched Cristina bring the candle toward her arm again. Why was she so weak?

She opened her mouth to scream again when the door banged against the frame causing both women to start.

But before Cordelia could even register what had happened, the candle went flying across the room, landing on the floor.

"What the—" The Countess stood, letting go of her arm. "You!"

"Me," Malice rumbled. "You've taken something of mine and I want it back."

Cristina's mouth curled into a sneer. "So like a man to think he owns a woman."

Cordelia began to push off the bed, trying to get to Chad. If she were in his arms, she was sure to be safe. He bent down and in one movement, scooped her up with one hand, holding out a pistol in the other. "I'm letting Daring deal with you."

Cristina let out a primal cry, hitting her own chest with her fist. "He will never come anywhere near me again. I'd rather die."

Cordelia blinked. She was half standing but mostly leaning against Chad, his strong arm supporting her. "What happened to you?"

"I don't want your pity." Cristina flung her arm back out. "You're a traitor to all womankind."

Cordelia tucked her head into Malice's arm. She didn't care what she was. She'd never been happier to be next to someone than she was here with Malice. Then her nose caught something funny.

Glancing over she realized the candle had caught the drapes on fire. "Chad!"

"Damn," he yelled and holding her still, crossed the room and yanked the drape from the rod, attempting to stomp it out. It nearly caught her dress on fire and she screamed, barely able to stay out of the way. Even worse, he didn't put out the flames, instead, they spread to the wall. "We've got to get out of here."

He turned to swing her in his arms.

"The Countess of Abernath is gone," she gasped as he cradled her against his body.

He leaned down and kissed her head. "We'll deal with her later." Then he started for the door.

Reaching the hall, he started for the back stairs.

"We have to warn everyone about the fire," she called as smoke began to fill the hall.

"We'll tell the staff about the fire in the kitchen if the countess hasn't already." He pulled her even closer. "My first priority is you."

His words made her insides go soft. For a man that claimed to have a cold heart, she realized their courtship had been straight from a story and now culminated with a daring rescue. A smile formed on her lips. If only he could declare his undying love. The smile slipped away. she'd have to content herself with a lovely fantasy.

A knocking noise from their right caught Cordelia's ear. "Chad. Did you hear that?"

"What," he kept sprinting toward the stairs.

She heard it again. "Stop." Cordelia hit his shoulder with all the strength she had left. "Someone's in there."

"Cordelia." He slowed. "I need to get you out—"

"Help," a tiny voice cried. "Please help. There's smoke."

"Chad," she begged, wiggling in his arms. "Is that a child?"

He stopped then and swung her down, leaning her against the wall. It was warm to the touch, which was terribly frightening. Chad tried the knob as the little voice cried again. "Back away from the door!" Chad yelled.

In one swift kick, he knocked the door near clean off its hinges. Standing there was a little golden-haired boy looking frightened and forlorn. Cordelia watched as Chad scooped the boy up in one arm then came back to her, wrapping another large arm about her. "Can you walk?"

"I have to," she answered, but just then, Daring came sprinting up the stairs.

"What the bloody hell?" he yelled but then grabbed the boy and turned back down the steps without another word.

"We have to warn the staff," Cordelia yelled to him.

"They know and they've mostly scattered already as far as I can tell." He pounded down the stairs. "Who am I carrying?"

"I'm Harry," the little boy said.

Daring bounced the boy more securely in his arms as he hit the bottom step and made a break for the back door. The stableman were already racing past them with buckets of water in hand. Reaching the outdoors, Daring didn't stop and neither did Chad as they made their way to a carriage parked in the alley. Daring opened the door and practically tossed Harry inside. Then he turned back to Chad. "You get them out of here, check them into the nearest inn. I'm going to help with the fire."

"Are you certain?" Chad was already stuffing her into the carriage. She made it in on wobbly legs and then collapsed onto a seat. "The Tuttleberry Inn is just down the street. Meet me there."

With a nod, Daring was off again, joining the bucket brigade.

Chad climbed in after her and snapped the door closed. "You're safe now."

Cordelia stared at the man who'd just staged her daring rescue. She wanted to throw herself in his arms and declare her undying love. But she held her tongue. "Thank you?"

He slid on the seat next to her and pulled her into his lap. "You're welcome."

She nibbled at her lip as she settled her face into the hollow of his neck. How to marry a man that she loved so deeply knowing he didn't return her affection?

CHAPTER SEVENTEEN

MALICE HELD Cordelia in his lap, the little boy sat on the other bench huddled in a ball, tears streaming down his face.

"Harry," he said softy. "Do you want to come sit with us?"

The boy launched off the bench, landing against Malice's side with a decided thud. In response, Malice wrapped an arm about him. "You're all right."

The boy turned a teary face up to him. "Do I have to go back?"

The boy's large blue eyes stared up at him, wide and full of fear. "Was that your home?" Had the Countess of Abernath kidnapped a child too?

The boy didn't speak for a few seconds and Cordelia shifted in his lap to hold the boy's hand. "It's all right. You can tell us."

"I've always lived with Lady Abernath." The boy swallowed.

Well that didn't explain very much. He hugged the child tighter. "We'll figure all of this out. For now, you are safe with us."

The carriage rumbled to a stop and Malice pulled out his two charges, hurrying them into the inn and securing a suite. Calling out a request for a breakfast tray, he ushered them upstairs and locked the door behind him.

Cordelia all but collapsed on a settee and the boy stood staring at her while hugging his chest.

She waved to him and, without hesitation, he hurried over. Opening her arms, he climbed into her embrace. "I had a teacher who was very kind to me," he said and then burrowed his head against her arm. "She was pretty like you too."

"A teacher?" she asked, closing her eyes but hugging him closer.

Malice's heart squeezed to see them curled together. This boy reminded him of himself. If only someone like Cordelia had been there then. Wrapped him in her arms.

The boy nodded. "She left a little while ago. But she said she'd try to come back for me." Harry tipped his head back. "The countess is very mean. Miss Pennyworth couldn't stay but she wanted to."

169

Cordelia's face spasmed and then she looked to him. Her eyes were scrunched as though she were pleading with him in some fashion. He knew what she wanted to ask, he wished to protect Harry too.

A knock came at the door and peering out, he saw a servant with a large tray of food. Quickly, he turned the lock and opened the door, taking the tray before he closed the room again.

They ate in silence, Harry eating a man's portion of food before he lay back down with Cordelia. In minutes both of them were sound asleep, wrapped together.

Nearly an hour passed before another knock sounded at the door. Rising he looked out the peephole to see Daring, looking rather sooty, standing on the other side.

He opened it again, letting his friend in. "You made it."

"I did." Daring removed his hat and wiped his brow. "Bloody mess that was."

"What happened?" Malice gestured toward the fireplace and both men crossed the room.

Daring turned his hat in his hand. "The countess has disappeared. The staff was able to get the fire out before it spread to more homes." Daring wiped his brow again. "Honestly, they seemed relieved to be free of her and I told them all to visit me tomorrow for recommendations for a new post."

"That's good," he answered, bracing his hand against the fireplace. He knew the worst news was yet to come.

"The housekeeper was especially chatty. It turns out that the boy..." Daring looked over to the child sleeping in Cordelia's arms. "Is Lady Abernath's child."

Malice sucked in his breath. He knew what Daring was thinking. Was this his child?

Daring looked down into the flames. "Lord Abernath made the boy his heir so he's an earl."

"How can he be the earl if Lord Abernath...." But he stopped.

"That's right. Abernath died six weeks ago at their country home. Lady Abernath has kept that fact along with the birth of the child a secret."

Malice scratched his head. "I wonder if the death of her husband is why she's suddenly reemerged in your life looking for revenge."

Daring nodded. "The housekeeper mentioned that not a penny of the money is hers. It all went to the boy. What little is left."

They both looked over at the sleeping child. "He's frightened out of his mind. We both know what sort of person she is."

"She's his mother. I don't know how you could take him away from her." His fist clenched. "Unless you could prove that someone else is his father?"

Malice leaned his head against the mantel. "That's a bloody mess, isn't it? Do you think he's yours? How would Minnie feel about this child becoming your heir and being part of your family?"

Daring shook his head. "It would better explain why Cristina is so angry with me. But then again she had more than one man in her bed. Including me, three that I know of."

Malice frowned. "The child looks nothing like you."

Daring stared at the boy. "No. He doesn't, and he's already got a title, but we also can't leave a tender child in her grips. The woman isn't sane."

"Well, for now, he can stay with me." Malice looked at him, his heart thudding in his chest. He never in his life thought he'd take on another child, not even his own, but here he was, his heart ready to give this boy love.

"Are you certain? It's a big commitment."

Malice nodded. "I wish someone had done this for me. Swooped in and rescued me from a man who hated the sight of my face."

Daring grimaced. "You're a good man, Lord Malicorn."

"Not Malice?" he raised a brow.

Daring stared back. "You're not that man anymore, are you?"

No. He supposed he wasn't. It was time he told Cordelia what she meant to him.

———

CORDELIA WOKE WITH A START. First, she had no idea where she was...again. Looking around the room, she realized it was well-appointed with rich mahogany and dark velvet drapes over the windows and the bed.

She sat up, pulling the covers with her. When had her clothes been removed? Her arm was still in the sling but everything else, besides her shift, was off.

It was dark. Had night fallen? Last she remembered; it had been morning hadn't it? Details on the night before came flooding back and she gasped as she remembered she'd been kidnapped.

"What's wrong?" a deep voice slurred next to her. "Bad dream?"

How had she not noticed she wasn't in bed alone? Glancing to her right, Chad blinked up at her. "I didn't know where I was."

He gave her a sleepy smile. "You're safe with me at the inn."

"The inn?" she asked. "What of my family?"

He covered her hand with his. "Daring sent them a message saying that you were safely recovered but so exhausted from your ordeal that you were sleeping here. Of course, your family thinks that Minnie and Daring are with us as chaperones but I won't tell if you don't."

"And Harry?" she asked settling back down on the bed.

He smiled and reached out to stroke her face. "Sleeping in the other room. The inn has graciously allowed me to hire a maid to stay with him."

She relaxed her shoulders. "That poor boy. He seems lost."

Malice drew in a deep breath. Hope gleamed in his eyes. "I'm hoping that you'll consent to giving him a new home with us."

Cordelia gasped. She lifted her hand to her heart, feeling it beat madly. "Is that even possible?"

"Well, considering you were just kidnapped by his mother, Daring is fairly certain he can have Lady Abernath committed. So I'd say yes, it's more than possible." Then he frowned. "If it's all right with you."

She rolled over to face him and without thought placed a kiss on his lips. "Of course it is. What a beautiful gift for you to give him." Then she kissed him again, her mouth pressing to his, making her insides soft and gooey. "You're a fine man, Chad Malicorn."

He held her face in his hands and gave her a long lingering kiss. "That is better than being suitable."

She wrinkled her nose. "Speaking of that." Her heart began to pound in her chest. "I know after what's happened you'll want to rescue me from any consequences from my abduction."

"There will be no consequences. We'll be married and no one will question—"

She placed a hand on his chest. "I don't think we should marry."

"What?" His brow drew together. "You've already accepted my proposal."

Cordelia licked her lips, trying to gain the courage to say the next part. "But you see. I love you. I'm in love with you."

He stared at her, not saying a word.

She trembled as she continued. "I can't marry you because it will break my heart to feel this way about you when you don't return my—"

But he didn't allow her to finish. Instead, his mouth covered hers in a searing kiss that stole the air from her lungs.

He slanted open her mouth and probed her tongue with his, making her groan in sweet desire as his body rolled on top of hers. He'd already removed his shirt and her hand roved along the bare muscles of his back, feeling every ridge and hollow. Finally he lifted up his head. "Corde, a man does not go around rescuing women, fighting opponents, and stealing kisses in gardens if he doesn't love her in return."

"What?" She pulled her head back deeper into the pillow to focus on his face. "You love me?"

He stroked her cheek with his thumb. "I love you as much as I love the warm rays of the sun on a summer day. As much as I love air, and blue sky, and fields of summer flowers."

Something deep inside her burst with joy to hear those words. Could it be true? "Are you waxing poetic?" Her tongue darted out again and he stared at it, his body tensing.

"I am, my little pixie." Then he slowly lowered himself down until his lips met hers again. "I love you so much I ache from it. I can't stand being apart from you." He slid his hand down her neck and over her chest until he cupped one of her breasts. Pleasure rocked through her and she arched into the touch. "If you let me, I'll spend my whole life proving to you just how much I love you."

He tweaked her nipple and she cried out, her legs

wrapping about his. "Yes," she murmured. Then repeated louder. "Oh yes."

He started kissing a trail down her neck as his other hand reached for the hem of her shift. It had already ridden up her legs and he ran his hand along her outer thigh, pushing the fabric higher. "How did I ever think I could remain detached from you?"

She couldn't answer as he skimmed his hand along her hip and then slid across her stomach, dipping lower until his fingertips brushed the curls at her apex. She could feel heat, warmth, and wet coming from her core and as he traced the outline of her sex and then dipped his fingers into her womanly flesh.

Her insides spasmed and she gasped, her eyes losing focus. "Chad," she begged not sure what she was asking for. He responded by leaning down and taking her taut nipple into his mouth. The cloth still separated his lips from her flesh but all the same, the peak tightened and puckered until she was writhing in pleasure under him.

He stopped, rising above her and she gave a little whimper of protest. She didn't want to stop. But he only took the hem of her shift and slid it up her chest and then over her head. When his chest came down on top of hers, she wanted to sigh in pleasure at the feel of his skin. "I love the way your hair feels," she whispered close to his ear. "Your fingers, your mouth. I didn't know it would all be so wonderful."

He kissed her lips again, his fingers gently stroking her sex once again. "It only gets better, love. I promise."

How could that be true?

CHAPTER EIGHTEEN

MALICE LOOKED down at the beautiful little pixie currently begging for his touch and tried not to roar with satisfaction. The noise he made was more like a guttural growl. This beautiful, magical woman was all his.

And she loved him too. That part still stunned him. He wasn't certain he deserved it, but he was done questioning his worth. Instead, he intended to spend his life attempting to be the man she needed him to be.

That was the only way. He understood that now.

He thought back to the night that she'd promised to heal the wounds buried deep inside him. She already had. Here he was, filled with love, his heart open, not only to her but to the boy who reminded him so much of himself.

Why hadn't he done this sooner?

"Cordelia," he said as he kissed her again. "I can't believe we're here."

She wrapped her arm about this neck. "Me either. You're certain you love me?"

He groaned as reached for the stays of his breeches. "Very," he answered. He pulled down his breeches, freeing his manhood.

She slid a hand down his body and reached between his legs, her light touch exploring his flesh and causing his teeth to clench. Her hand felt bloody amazing. "And we're going to marry?" she asked again. "You don't mind I'm a writer?"

Her hand dipped lower, cupping his sack and his eyes rolled back in his head. "I love it."

"I'm quiet. And people don't notice me at balls or—"

"Cordelia." His teeth clenched. "You're holding my balls in your hand."

She let out a tiny gasp and then a giggle. "I am."

He touched his forehead to hers. "Never has a woman been this deep inside me before. You might be quiet and shy, but you have managed to touch me in places I thought long dead."

"Oh," she said, her sweet breath blowing across his face. "That is beautiful." Then she arched to kiss him and the head of his manhood slid against her soft wet sex.

He throbbed with need. "You are beautiful. Never let anyone take that away from you again." The tip slid inside her folds, wrapping a tight wet heat about his cock. He began to shake, the effort of going slow becoming increasingly difficult.

"You're beautiful too," she whispered against his lips. "I meant what I said a few days ago. I'll spend my life showing you what it means to be loved if you let me."

He couldn't hold back. Those words opening him wide. He slid inside her, feeling her maidenhead tear under the pressure. She gave a cry of pain, her body stiffening. "I'm sorry love."

"Don't be," she said. "We're one now."

They were. And they would be forever. He began to move inside her, slowly, allowing her body to adjust. When she relaxed in his arms, he began to move more quickly. If she'd been hesitant at first, with each stroke, she grew bolder and more confident, her rhythm building faster and tighter.

How could lovemaking be this good? But he couldn't say the words out loud. He could only hold her close as they climbed higher, their bodies truly becoming one.

"Cordelia," he cried, holding her close. "I love you so much."

"I love you, too," she returned, her body spasming around him. He couldn't take another moment and his seed filled her. She was truly his now.

And she would be forever. No one would take her away from him, and he knew deep in his heart she'd never abandon him.

He collapsed on the bed, drawing her close. "We need to move up the wedding."

"I beg your pardon," she asked, already snuggling deeply into his side.

"I can't wait a month to be with you again. We need to marry now." He pulled her tighter to his body.

She let out a sleepy giggle. "Finally something involving men that I am good at."

He turned her face. "As far as I am concerned, you've been good at all of it from the first moment you fell into my arms."

She nuzzled his side. "Well, since you've put it that way, we'll have to move up the wedding. Considering that I was kidnapped yesterday, I'm sure my mother will agree."

"Good God, do I owe the Countess of Abernath a debt of gratitude?"

She lifted her head. "I don't know about that but you are definitely getting softer."

He leaned down and kissed her forehead. "It's all your fault. By the time you're done I'm going to be helping you write romances while collecting children and puppies in my spare time."

"I've never heard anything sexier in my life." Then she let out a sigh. "How can I be so tired after sleeping all day?"

"Rest love," he answered. "Tomorrow, we'll begin the rest of our lives."

EPILOGUE

CORDELIA STOOD at the back of her family's church, staring at her groom who beamed back at her, extending his arm.

She'd considered not wearing her glasses but he'd gifted her with a new pair. They truly fit her face better, and now she could see his expression. Soft and happy, it spoke of all the feelings she too felt. She wouldn't have wanted to miss that for all the world.

She barely touched the floor as she floated toward him. It had only been two days since they'd returned from the inn, but she'd began another life that day. In this one, she was Cordelia the writer and wife and maker of passionate romance.

In fact, Chad had spent the last two days convincing her to send her earlier stories to a publisher. They would be under an assumed name, of course. Sharing them filled her with excitement for the first time in her life. Chad had said something had shifted in him. The same was true for her. She grew more confident with each passing day. She had her soon-to-be husband to thank for that.

Someone clapped to her left and she looked over to see Harry sitting next to her mother. The boy beamed back.

With a tiny wave she finished her march down the aisle and placed her hand in Chad's.

The ceremony filled her with joy and light and as her hands clasped her husband's, the bond between them swelled. As long as she lived, she'd remember this day.

"Chad," she said, leaning close. "This is better than any book I've ever read."

"I agree." He squeezed her hands. "But I've every confidence you'll write a better one."

That made her heart swell in her chest and she could barely breathe as they exchanged their vows.

Finally, the service ended and Chad leaned over, sealing their union with a kiss. The room burst into applause and Cordelia looked out over their family and friends and nearly yelled in surprise.

At the very back of the room sat Emily and Jack. "They're home."

"Bloody hell, they are." Then Chad cleared his throat. "Apologies, Father."

The priest nodded and Cordelia and Chad started down the aisle, making their way through the doors and into the waiting carriage. They would return to her parents' home for the wedding breakfast.

"I'm so glad my sister made it for my wedding after all." Cordelia gave her husband's hand a pat.

He grimaced. "I want to know why they left in the first place."

She shook her head. "I'm sure they had a good reason."

The carriage stopped and they stepped out onto the steps waiting as each of the guests arrived. Her parents came next along with Grace and Diana. Minnie and Daring just after them. Her aunt and Ada arrived after that. Emily and Jack were the last carriage to enter the drive. All the guests turned to them as they made their way to the door.

"Let's step inside first, shall we?" Jack grimaced as he reached for Emily's hand.

Silently the crowd entered the house. Emily pushed to the front of the group, reaching for Cordelia's arm.

"Corde, I'm sorry. I didn't mean to disrupt your

wedding." Emily cringed. "I just didn't want to miss it."

"I don't care about that." Cordelia reached for her sister. "I just want to know, we all want to know what happened."

Jack came to stand next to his wife. "It's my fault."

"Why?" Chad asked, squinting his eyes.

Jack grimaced. "The shortest version is that Emily was threatened by the Countess of Abernath. I didn't want to wait another month for our wedding and I wanted to get away from London. What I didn't realize was that by leaving, she'd focus her attention on someone like Cordelia instead."

"How do you know all of this?" Cordelia asked.

Both Jack and Emily looked to Daring. The duke cleared his throat. "I've been writing them." He shrugged. "Two weddings have happened since they left."

Diana stepped up to the group. "Tell me that all your friends aren't planning to propose to my family." Her arms crossed over her chest. "I've no intention of marrying, especially not one of your group."

Daring lifted a brow. "I'm sure you're safe. But I'm curious to know what was in that letter that spooked you so."

Jack ran his hand through his hair. "To tell you

that, I have to confess some other sins to you and I'm not sure how you'll react."

Daring straightened. "We'll find out, won't we?"

Jack gave a nod. "Let's have this conversation with all the men. They should know too."

"Fine." Daring gave a terse nod. "We'll keep it short, however. Malice has a new bride to attend. Shall we say five tonight?"

"Five it is…"

EARL OF EXILE
Lords of Scandal Book 3

Tammy Andresen

EARL OF EXILE

LORDS OF SCANDAL BOOK 3

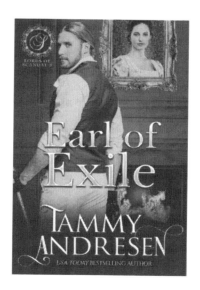

Lord Callum Exmouth stood on the edge of the large ball room, strategically placed by one of the open garden doors. The spring breeze kept the air around him fresh and made him feel less trapped by the crowd. Large social gatherings made him uncomfortable. Not that he couldn't participate in them, he just didn't like them.

He rolled his neck from side to side, causing it to crack. Hell, he hated parties and balls. Unlike the other men in his circle, he hadn't grown up knowing he was part of the peerage. His friends called him Exile, and the name suited him. He was an outcast, especially among his own family.

A gentleman bumped him and Exile let out a deep rumble of dissatisfaction. The man looked over at him, his brow scrunched until he caught Exile's gaze then his own eyes widened in surprise. "I beg your pardon." The man shuffled off quickly giving several worried glances backward.

He cracked two of his knuckles as if to underscore his point. Exile had that effect on people. His sheer size was intimidating.

Exile's cousin, Ewan, was supposed to be the next Earl of Exmouth. Ewan had been born and raised for the position of one Scottish earl and had taken to the role naturally. Fair and decent, Ewan would have made an excellent leader of his people. Exile thought back to his larger than life cousin. Though, physically speaking, they'd been the same size, even as kids, Ewan had always known what to do. One summer, Exile had stayed with his aunt and uncle on their estate north of Glasgow. While playing with a group of boys, one of them had fallen from a tree and broken his arm. At twelve years of age, Ewan had taken charge. He'd sent one child for help, another was to hold the boy's hand, a third was to go directly to the doctor. Exile at ten had wondered if he'd ever be as capable as Ewan. Now at eight and twenty he was still asking himself that same question.

Two ladies passed by him, gossiping loudly. "Did you see the cut of her dress? Awful."

"I know," the other replied, snapping open her fan and giving him a long stare over the top.

Exile looked away, not interested. His mind was elsewhere in the past. More and more he thought of his cousin rather than less. Ewan should be the earl now. Instead, Ewan had died five years prior. The worst part was his cousin had left this world attempting, as usual, to do the right thing. Exile's gut clenched. Bloody unfair. So now, his family, his people were stuck with Exile as their earl. No one was happy about it. Certainly not his aunt. Definitely not the farmers who grumbled about how much time he spent in England and most certainly not himself.

Exile had never wanted the responsibility. Of

course, he still tried to do the best he could. Hell, he'd even gone into business running a gaming hell to make sure his people remained fed. Not that anyone would appreciate his efforts if they knew the truth. They'd likely call him morally corrupt. His aunt had outright told him, he wasn't the man Ewan had been on several occasions. She wasn't wrong. In fact, Exile mostly agreed.

He shifted, uncomfortable with where his thoughts had dragged him. A woman with a large feathered hat stepped in front of him, the plumes reaching several feet in the air and blocking his view. As he moved, he caught sight of the door. His friend, and fellow club owner walked into the room. The Duke of Darlington, being a full head taller than everyone else, was easy to spot. Next to him was his wife, Minnie. Her bright red hair also standing out in the crowd. He searched just behind her and saw the woman he'd originally come to see. Lady Diana Chase.

His insides tightened. He hadn't meant to react like that. He'd gone to the ball to see her, yes but not to be with her. In fact, he already had an intended, though he hadn't chosen that woman either. Fiona was Ewan's fiancée and his aunt was convinced that Exile should honor the commitment. If he recalled, her exact words were to the effect of, "It's the least ye could do."

His chest puffed out as he drew in a long breath. Marry a woman he'd never even met? Then again, after all the losses his aunt had endured, he wasn't certain how he could refuse.

He gazed down at Diana, his body clenching with awareness. He'd met her a month ago when she and her sisters had arrived at the illicit club in the middle of the night. Diana's sister, Emily had been in search of her fiancée. But the ladies had put both their reputations and the club's secret nature at risk by going there. Even worse, one of Darlington's enemies knew the ladies had been there.

As a result, Exile and his friends had agreed to keep watch over the Chase women. Make sure they didn't expose their secret or run into trouble themselves. A promise Exile couldn't regret more. Every time he looked at Diana, his breath froze in his chest like a bloody school boy with his first crush.

Darlington caught sight of Exile and headed straight for him. Inside Exile swore a string of curses. He should have refused to come here tonight. Should have stayed home. But he'd made a promise and the stakes of that promise had gotten more serious the past few days.

"You came," Darlington rumbled as he reached out his hand to shake Exile's.

Exile gave a single nod, making certain not to look at Diana. "Aye. I came."

"I suppose you're both worried after the incident with Cordelia..." Diana spoke from his left.

He still didn't look at her but that didn't stop her voice from vibrating through him. It was stronger and more confident than many women's but beautifully musical with high rich tones. The sound struck a chord deep inside him.

He turned toward her then, his heart stopping as he looked into those deep, dark brown eyes, fringed with long black lashes. She was tall for a woman, allowing him to really drink in the details of her face as he, himself was well over six feet. Her straight nose was punctuated by the tiniest upturn at the end, her full lips begged to be kissed, her high cheekbones only accentuating that fact.

Diana's dark hair was piled atop her head in a soft coif that made him long to touch the strands and he gripped his thigh to keep his hand in place. "Can't be too careful," he murmured, still drinking in every detail. Her dress came well off the shoulder, exposing her delicate skin and showing her cleavage. He'd like to kiss a path down her neck and over her shoulder, cutting across her chest and—

"With the Countess of Abernath loose about London, we must be very careful when we're out in public," Darlington spoke in a low voice, bending his head so as not to be overheard. He likely needn't have bothered, the room was so loud, Exile could barely hear himself think.

"Let's step outside. We'll be able to hear each other out there." Minnie wrapped her arm through her husband's and they both moved toward the open doors.

Exile had no choice but to hold out his elbow to Diana. As her delicate fingers slipped into his elbow, he flexed the muscles in his arm attempting to curb his reaction to her touch. "Did Cordelia and Malice successfully leave for Dover?"

Diana nodded. "They did. Cordelia seemed very relieved to have left London after what the countess did."

Exile grimaced. Darlington's former fiancée, the Countess of Abernath had stolen Cordelia from her own home. She'd been attempting to blackmail Cordelia into exposing the club and Darlington's involvement. "Can't say that I blame her. I'm surprised ye've come out at all."

Diana shrugged. "Ada and Grace are at home. But we need to make public appearances or society will begin to wonder what's happened to us and I'm most suited to stand in for the family."

His shoulder's straightened as he stared at her, admiration filling his chest. "Ye're a verra strong lass."

She looked up at him then, a small smile curving her lips. "I'll take that as a compliment. Thank you."

"I meant it as a compliment. Ye're welcome." She was just the sort of woman a Scottish man would like to walk beside. Strong, beautiful, ready to speak her mind and fight for the ones she loved.

And she could never be his.

———

Diana gave the large Scot next to her a sidelong glance. The man was interesting, she'd give him that. He was large, not fat, but tall and thickly muscled. He had broad features that would never work for a woman, but looked handsome on a man. His square jaw and heavily corded neck gave him an air of power and physical presence.

He was the sort of man a weaker woman might want to hide behind. Diana didn't hide from anything.

"The question, now that we've decided I'm of strong stock, is what does a man do with such a dominant woman?" She wasn't sure why she asked except that most men were a bit afraid of her. But not him. He looked right at her. In fact, his gaze was so strong, she often found herself shifting uncomfortably.

Exile swallowed, his Adam's apple bobbing. Then he mumbled so softly she almost didn't hear him, "I can think of a thing or two."

She nearly tripped over her own feet. She'd known that he was attracted to her from their first meeting. When they were together, his eyes never left her. But men often were enamored with her beauty until they got to know her better.

One man had made her believe he'd liked her just the way she was but he turned out to be a liar on so many levels. She supposed she should give Exile a few points for honesty but his innuendo reminded her that she wasn't dealing with a gentleman. Exile, just like the cad in her past, Charles Crusher, was a rogue. And once a rogue, always a rogue.

"Can you now?" she asked, stopping. Minnie and Darlington were just ahead. "Such a gentleman."

He grimaced, coming to a stop as well. "My apologies," He turned toward her. "I didna mean to offend."

His brogue tickled her ears, sliding down her neck. "You're not the first to make such insinuations and you won't be the last." She turned forward to begin walking again. "I don't pay any of you any mind."

He held her in place, not moving. "I'm just like those other men am I?" His voice had dropped deeper, lower, almost sinister. "Would those other men follow ye from ball to ball to keep ye safe?"

Diana raised her brows, giving him a long look. Why did part of her like this protective behavior? "Is that what you're doing?"

He shrugged. "Perhaps."

Diana gave her head a shake. "If that is, in fact, your real motive, I don't need you to follow me about, Lord Exmouth. Continue with your life and leave me to mine."

"I can't." His other hand came to her waist. Tingling heat spread through her at the touch. "I've made a promise and though I'm not as good a man as I'd like to be, I do keep my word."

What did that mean? He wasn't as good a man as he wanted to be? "I'm sure you do. I pride myself on needing no one's help."

He gave his head a shake. "Forgive me for stating the obvious but a lady doesn't have much choice in the matter."

"I have choices," she answered, notching up her chin. Unlike many women, she had money of her own that her mother and father had set aside for her. Perhaps she'd travel the world or open a bookstore. It didn't matter as long she wasn't subverted to someone else's will. "Enough of them, anyhow."

"Do tell," he answered. Darlington and Minnie had stopped just ahead and turned back to look at them.

"You're falling behind," Minnie called. "Shall we stay here and chat or should we walk a bit? I find I don't wish to go back to the party just yet."

"Let's walk," Exile answered.

Diana prickled, her spine snapping straighter. She didn't need him to talk for her. "I think--" she started but suddenly she lurched to the side as he gave her a push. Exile then grabbed her waist and righted her but Minnie and Darlington had already begun walking. She stopped, stomping her slipper on the stone path. "You did that on purpose."

"Guilty," he answered. "We're not done talking."

"I say we are done," she hissed back.

"Do you think you'll marry?" he asked, ignoring her completely.

The man was thick. Not physically, well technically he was very well muscled, but at this moment she meant mentally. And why was he prodding like this? It was a raw subject for her. "It's none of your business but I doubt it very much." Why was he asking such a question?

His hand at her waist tightened and he drew her closer. "Ye…unmarried?"

Her breath caught as his heat began to seep in through her dress. She tsked, looking up at him. "You don't know anything about me."

"I know a few things," he said, dropping his face closer to hers. "I know yer blood sings with passion. I can feel it even now."

She opened her mouth to answer but no words came out. He was right, of course and her passionate nature had gotten her into a fair bit of trouble already. "You're wrong."

"I'm not." His mouth dropped even closer to hers. "I can prove it too."

"How?" Had she just asked that out loud? Why had she done that? But she already knew. She was attracted to him, the rapid beat of her heart affirmed that fact with every thump. And part of her, the very bad part, wanted what he was about to do.

By way of answer, he dropped his mouth to hers, his lips pressing hers closed. Fire and heat, and sweet stinging passion shot through her veins, making her gasp in delight. He lifted his mouth again but only for a moment before he kissed her again and then a third time, each building the tension in her body until she wanted to crush herself against that large chest.

What had she just done?

Want to read more? Earl of Exile

Read the entire Lords of Scandal series!

Duke of Daring
    Marquess of Malice
    Earl of Exile
    Viscount of Vice
    Baron of Bad
    Earl of Sin

ABOUT THE AUTHOR

Tammy Andresen lives with her husband and three children just outside of Boston, Massachusetts. She grew up on the Seacoast of Maine, where she spent countless days dreaming up stories in blueberry fields and among the scrub pines that line the coast. Her mother loved to spin a yarn and Tammy filled many hours listening to her mother retell the classics. It was inevitable that at the age of eighteen, she headed off to Simmons College, where she studied English literature and education. She never left Massachusetts but some of her heart still resides in Maine and her family visits often.

Find out more about Tammy:
http://www.tammyandresen.com/
https://www.facebook.com/authortammyandresen
https://twitter.com/TammyAndresen
https://www.pinterest.com/tammy_andresen/
https://plus.google.com/+TammyAndresen/

Read Tammy Andresen's other books:

Seeds of Love: Prequel to the Lily in Bloom series

Lily in Bloom

Midnight Magic

Keep up with all the latest news, sales, freebies, and releases by joining my newsletter!

www.tammyandresen.com

Hugs!

OTHER TITLES BY TAMMY

Boxed sets!!

Taming the Duke's Heart Books 1-3

Taming the Duke's Heart Books 4-6

A Laird to Love Books 1-3

A Laird to Love Books 4-6

Wicked Lords of London Books 1-3

Wicked Lords of London Books 4-6

Wicked Lords of London

Earl of Sussex

My Duke's Seduction

My Duke's Deception

My Earl's Entrapment

My Duke's Desire

My Wicked Earl

New: Taming the Duke's Heart
    Taming a Defiant Duke
    Taming a Wicked Rake
    Taming an Unrepentant Earl
    Taming my Christmas (Coming in November of
2019)

How to Reform a Rake
    How to Reform a Rake
    Don't Tell a Duke You Love Him
    Meddle in a Marquess's Affairs
    Never Trust an Errant Earl
    Never Kiss an Earl at Midnight
    Make a Viscount Beg

Brethren of Stone
    The Duke's Scottish Lass
    Scottish Devil
    Wicked Laird
    Kilted Sin
    Rogue Scot
    The Fate of a Highland Rake

A Laird to Love
    Christmastide with my Captain (FREE!!!)
    My Enemy, My Earl
    Heart of a Highlander

A Scot's Surrender
My Laird's Seduction
The Earl's Forsaken Bride

Taming the Duke's Heart

Taming a Duke's Reckless Heart (FREE!! Check it out today!)
Taming a Duke's Wild Rose
Taming a Laird's Wild Lady
Taming a Rake into a Lord
Taming a Savage Gentleman
Taming a Rogue Earl

Printed by Amazon Italia Logistica S.r.l.
Torrazza Piemonte (TO), Italy

12673822R00125